The Mystery of
Holly Lane

The Eleventh Adventure of
the Five Find-Outers and
Buster the Dog

P9-DCA-220

Also by Enid Blyton in the Mystery series

Enid Blyton

The Mystery of
Holly Lane

The Eleventh Adventure of the Five
Find-Outers and Buster the Dog

A DRAGON BOOK

GRANADA
London Toronto Sydney New York

Published by Granada Publishing Limited
in 1969
Reprinted 1970, 1971, 1972, 1973, 1974, 1975, 1976
1977, 1979, 1980

ISBN 0 583 30125 8

First published by Methuen & Co Ltd 1953
Copyright © Enid Blyton 1953

Granada Publishing Limited
Frogmore, St Albans, Herts AL2 2NF
and
3 Upper James Street, London W1R 4BP
866 United Nations Plaza, New York, NY 10017, USA
117 York Street, Sydney, NSW 2000, Australia
100 Skyway Avenue, Rexdale, Ontario, M9W 3A6, Canada
PO Box 84165, Greenside, 2034 Johannesburg, South Africa
61 Beach Road, Auckland, New Zealand

Granada ®
Granada Publishing ®

Printed in Canada

"Bets — don't gobble your porridge like that!" said Mrs. Hilton. "There's no hurry, surely!"

"Well, there is, Mother," said Bets. "I've got to go and meet Fatty's train this morning. Have you forgotten that he's coming home today?"

"But he's not arriving till the middle of the morning, is he?" said her mother. "There's plenty of time. Please don't gobble like that."

"I expect Bets wants to go and lay a red carpet down for Fatty, and get a band to play to welcome him," said her brother Pip, with a grin. "That's what you're in a hurry about, aren't you, Bets? Got to go and round up the band and see that all their instruments are polished!"

"Don't be so *silly*," said Bets, crossly, and tried to kick him under the table. He dodged his legs out of the way and she kicked her father's ankle instead. He put down his paper and glared.

"Oh, Dad — I'm sorry!" said Bets. "Please I'm very sorry. I meant to kick Pip. You see . . ."

"Any more of this kind of behaviour at breakfast-time and you can both go out of the room," said Mr. Hilton, and raised his paper again, leaning it against the big milk-jug. There was a dead silence for a minute or two except for the sound of spoons in the porridge bowls.

"Are you both going to meet Fatty?" asked Mrs. Hilton at last.

"Yes," said Bets, glad to have the silence broken. "But I want to go round and collect Buster first. Fatty asked me to. That's why I'm in a hurry."

5

"I suppose you're going to give old Buster a bath, and then dry him, and then brush him, and then tie a red ribbon round his neck," said Pip. "Well, well – that will take half the morning, certainly. Are you going to wear your best dress to meet Fatty, Bets?"

"I think you're horrid this morning," said Bets, almost in tears. "I should have thought you'd be pleased to meet Fatty, too. It's maddening that his school should have broken up after Easter, instead of before, like ours did. It means we'll go back before he does."

Pip stopped teasing Bets. "Yes, it's a silly idea, some schools breaking up before Easter and some after. I'm coming to meet Fatty too, of course, and I'll go and collect Buster with you. I'll even help you to bath him."

"I wasn't *going* to bath him," said Bets. "You know I wasn't. Pip – do you suppose Fatty will be in disguise – just to have a joke with us?"

"I hope to goodness you are not going to get mixed up in any nonsense again these holidays," said her father, entering suddenly into the conversation again. "I'm getting tired of having that fat policeman, Mr. Goon, round here complaining of this and that. As soon as that boy Frederick appears on the scene something always seems to happen."

"Well, Fatty can't help it," said Bets loyally. "I mean – mysteries keep *on* happening, Dad, you can't stop them. The papers are full of them."

"There's absolutely need for you to be mixed up in so many," said her father. "That boy Frederick – or Fatty as you so rightly call him – ought not to poke his nose into them. Leave them to the police!"

"Oh, but Fatty's *much* cleverer than our policeman, Mr. Goon," said Bets. "Anyway, I don't expect there will be time for anything exciting these hols."

Pip changed the subject quickly. He didn't want his

6

father suddenly to forbid him and Bets to have anything to do with any possible new mystery, as he had done once before. He had a kind of feeling that that was what would happen if he didn't hurriedly change the subject!

"Dad – the gardener is still away," he said. "Is there anything you want me to do in the garden, just to help out?"

Mr. Hilton looked pleased. "Ah – I wondered if you were going to suggest giving a bit of help," he said. "Now, you come into my study before I go and I'll give you a list of jobs I'd like done. They'll keep you out of mischief anyway!"

Pip heaved a sigh of relief. He didn't particularly want to do any gardening, but at least he had headed his father off the subject of Mysteries. It would have been dreadful if he had been forbidden to take part in any during the three weeks that were left of the holidays. He gave Bets a frown to make her understand she was not to mention Fatty again.

After breakfast Pip disappeared into the study with his father. He came up to Bets later, as she was making her bed. He looked rather rueful.

"Look at this list! Whew! Dad must think I'm a super-gardener! I'll never do all this."

Bets looked at the list. "Please go and do some now," she said. "You don't want to spend all the afternoon doing it – Fatty might want us to go to tea, or something. I wish I could help you. I'll make your bed and tidy your room, anyway. Will you be ready to start at twenty to eleven, Pip? Fatty's train gets in just before eleven, and I *must* collect Buster."

Pip heaved a mournful sigh as he looked at his list of jobs once more. "All right. I'll go and start now. Thanks for saying you'll do my bed and tidy up. See you later!"

At twenty to eleven Bets went out into the garden to find Pip. He was just putting a rake away, and looked extremely hot. "Is it time?" he called. "Gosh, I've been working like ten gardeners rolled into one."

"You look as if you're going to burst into flame at any minute," said Bets, with a giggle. "You'd better wash your hands, they're filthy. I'll go on ahead and collect Buster. Don't be long!"

She ran down the drive happily. She was tremendously glad that Fatty was coming back at last. Bets was very fond of him. She thought he must be the cleverest, most ingenious and certainly the kindest boy in the world. The things he could do!

"Those disguises of his! And the way he thinks out things – and the daring things he does!" she thought, as she turned out of the front gate and up the lane. "Oh, I'm *glad* Fatty's coming back. Things are always dull without him. It's quite true what Dad said – things do begin to happen when Fatty is around!"

Somebody whistled loudly when she got into the main road and she turned quickly. It was Larry, with Daisy, his sister. They waved madly and began to run.

"Are you going to meet Fatty? So are we! Where is Pip? Isn't he coming?"

Bets explained. "I'm on my way to collect Buster," she said. "Pip's just coming. Won't old Buster be pleased to see Fatty? I bet he knows it's the day he's arriving."

"I bet he does," agreed Larry. "He'll be waiting for us, his tongue out, panting to go!"

But oddly enough, Buster was not waiting. Mrs. Trotteville, Fatty's mother, was picking daffodils in the garden when the three children came up. She smiled at them.

"Going to meet Fatty? It will be nice to have him back, won't it?"

"Yes, very," said Larry. "Where's Buster, Mrs. Trotteville? We thought we'd take him along."

"In the kitchen, I think," said Mrs. Trotteville. "I haven't

8

seen him for a little while. He would keep treading all over the daffodils, so I sent him in."

Larry, Daisy and Bets went to the kitchen door and called loudly. "Buster! Hey, BUSTER! Come along, we're going to meet Fatty!"

But no Buster appeared. There was no scamper of short, eager legs, no welcoming volley of barks. The cook came to the door.

"He's not here," she said. "He did come in a minute or two ago, but off he went again. He's probably gone off with the baker's boy. He likes him, goodness knows why. He's a cheeky little monkey, that boy."

"Well – we'll have to go without Buster," said Larry, disappointed. "How maddening of him to go off just at this time. Fatty will be disappointed."

They set off to the station, joined by a breathless Pip. "Where's Buster? Don't say he's gone off just when we want him! Not at all like Buster!"

They hurried on. "Do you suppose Fatty will play a joke on us and turn up in disguise?" said Bets. "I do hope he doesn't. I just want to see him nice and fat and grinning all over his face."

"We shall be jolly late if we don't hurry," said Larry, looking at his watch. "Look – isn't that the train coming in now – and we're not nearly there. Buck up!"

They bucked up, and arrived at the station just as the train began to pull out again. The passengers had got out and were now walking down the platform. Two or three were waiting with their luggage for a porter.

"Look – there's old Buster!" said Pip, suddenly. "Would you believe it! Sitting under that seat – look – all by himself, watching."

Sure enough, there was the little Scottie, patiently waiting there. "How did he know that Fatty's train was due now?" said Bets, in wonder. "However DID he know! So that's where he ran off to – the station! He was on time too, and we weren't. Clever old Buster!"

"Where's Fatty?" said Daisy, as the crowd of passengers came up to the door where the ticket-collector stood. "I can't see him yet."

"He *may* be in disguise – just to test us and see how bright we are," said Pip. "Look at every one very carefully – especially people with glasses."

They stood silently behind the collector as every one surged past, giving up tickets. A big, bustling woman – a pair of schoolgirls – a man with a bag – two young soldiers in khaki, each with enormous kit-bags on their shoulders – two men bundled up in thick overcoats, both wearing glasses. Was one Fatty? They were both about his build. One said something in a foreign language as he passed by.

The four children stared after him doubtfully. He *could* be Fatty. They turned to watch the rest of the passengers, but there was no one who could possibly be Fatty.

At the end came Buster, all alone. Bets patted him, thinking that he looked sad. "So you missed him too, did you?" she said. "Buster, was he one of those bundled-up men?"

There was now no one left on the platform except a porter. "Come on," said Larry, making up his mind. "Fatty *must* have been one of those men. We'll follow them. We can't have old Fatty tricking us as easily as this!"

A Little Bit of Help!

The four children went out of the station and looked up the road. Where had the men gone?

"There they are," said Larry. "Look – just at the corner!"

"But who's the man with Fatty?" said Pip, puzzled. "He

10

never said anything about coming back with somebody."

"Look – they've shaken hands," said Daisy. "I expect old Fatty just fell into conversation with him to trick us a bit more. Come on – I'm sure the man who's gone off to the right is Fatty. He's got his walk, somehow."

"And he's going in the right direction," said Pip. "It's Fatty all right."

They hurried after him. When they got to the corner they paused. Now, where was he?"

"There he is – talking to that woman," said Larry. "Hurry!"

They hurried. The man, his coat-collar turned up, wearing thick glasses over his eyes, was saying something very earnestly to a thin little woman with a shopping-basket.

The four came up behind him and listened with amusement. Oh Fatty, Fatty!

"I seek my sistair's house. You will tell me, pliss? The house, it is called Grintriss."

"Never heard of it," said the woman, looking most suspiciously at the bundled-up man.

"Pardon? Where is zis house?" asked the man anxiously.

"I said, 'NEVER HEARD OF IT,'" said the woman. "There's no house called Grintriss that I know of. What's your sister's name?"

"Her name is Françoise Emilie Harris," said the man, going suddenly very French.

"Never heard of her either," said the thin little woman, looking more suspicious than ever. "Why don't you ask at the post-office?"

"Pliss? What is zis postoffis?" began the man, but the woman walked off impatiently, leaving him standing there with his bag.

Pip nudged Larry. "This is where we come in," he said, in a low voice. "We'll tell old Fatty we know where his sister lives, and that we'll take him there – and we'll lead him straight to his own house. That'll show him we've seen through him! Come on."

"Where's his school trunk?" said Bets, pulling Pip back as he started off after the man. "Are you *sure* it's Fatty?"

"He's sent his trunk carriage forward, of course," said Pip. "Come on – *look* at that walk – it's exactly like old Fatty's."

They set off after the man. Daisy suddenly thought of something. Where was Buster? She looked round but he wasn't there.

"What happened to Buster?" she said. "Surely he didn't stay behind? I was just wondering why *he* didn't know it was Fatty, and dash round his legs."

"He would have, if he'd been with us," said Pip. "He didn't recognize him in that crowd at the station and he's probably patiently sitting under the seat again, waiting!"

"Oh, poor Buster!" said Bets. "Look – Fatty has stopped another woman. What a scream he is!"

The second woman had no patience. She just shook her head and hurried off. Larry put his fingers to his mouth and let off a piercing whistle, making the others jump.

"Don't," said Daisy. "You know you're not allowed to do that. It's a horrible noise and makes people awfully angry."

"It's stopped old Fatty, anyway," said Larry, pleased. "Look, he's turned round."

"He's gone on again," said Bets, with a giggle. "Let's catch him up. He's going the wrong way home now."

They hurried after the man. "We'll pretend we don't know it's Fatty," said Pip. "We'll make him think *he's* deceiving *us* – but we'll have the laugh all right, when we take him to his own house instead of to his mythical 'sistair's' house."

They caught up the man, and he stopped, peering at them through thick glasses. He had a small black mous-

12

tache. His coat-collar was turned up, and not much could be seen of his face.

"Ah! Some children! You will help me, yes?" said the man. "I look for my sistair's house."

"Vous cherchez la maison de votre soeur?" said Pip, in his best French. The man beamed at him.

"Oui, oui! It is called Grintriss."

"Grintriss! Oh, yes, we know where *that* is," said Larry, most untruthfully, playing up to Fatty for all he was worth. "This way, please. *Every*body knows Grintriss. A very nice house. Big one, too."

"Beeg? No, my sistair's house is leetle," said the man. "Vairy, vairy leetle. Grintriss it is called."

"Oh, yes. Grintriss. Vairy leetle," said Pip. "Er – do you feel the cold, Monsieur? You are well wrapped up."

"I have had the bad cold," said the man, and he sniffed, and gave a hollow cough. "I come to my sistair for a leetle holyday."

"Holiday, you mean?" said Daisy, and the four of them began to laugh. "That's a nasty little cough you've got. Very nasty."

The man coughed again, and Bets began to giggle. Didn't Fatty know they were pulling his leg? How often had she heard Fatty cough like that when he was disguised as some poor old man?

They all went up the road together, the man hunched up in his bulky coat. He pulled his scarf over his chin as they met the wind at a corner.

"We are soon at Grintriss?" he asked, anxiously. "This wind is too – too –"

"Too windy?" said Pip, obligingly. "That's the worst of winds. They're always so windy."

The man gave him a sudden stare and said no more. Larry guided him round the next corner and over the road

13

to Fatty's own house. Mrs. Trotteville was nowhere to be seen. Larry winked at Pip.

"We'll take him up to the front door and leave him there," he said, falling behind to whisper. "We'll just see what old Fatty says then!"

They marched him in firmly at the gate and right up to the front door. "Here you are," said Pip. "Grintriss! I expect your sistair will answer the door herself. I'll pull the bell for you."

He pulled the bell and banged on the knocker too. Then the four of them retreated to the front gate to see what Fatty would do. Would he swing round, take off his glasses and grin at them? Would he say "One up to you! You win!"

The door opened, and the house parlour-maid stood there. An argument seemed to arise, though the children couldn't hear all of it. The maid raised her voice.

"I said, 'there's no one here of that name. And what's more I've never heard of a house called Grintriss, either.'"

Bets suddenly heard quick footsteps coming up the road, and then a familiar bark. She ran through the gate, sure that it was Buster's bark.

She gave a shrill scream. "Buster! FATTY! It's Fatty! Oh, Fatty, then that wasn't you after all! FATTY!"

She rushed down the road and flung herself into Fatty's arms. There he was, as plump as ever, his eyes laughing, his mouth in a wide grin.

"Fatty! That wasn't you, then? Oh, dear!"

"What's all this about?" asked Fatty, swinging Bets into the air and down again. "Gosh, Bets, you're getting heavy. I soon shan't be able to do that. Why weren't you at the station to meet me? Only Buster was there."

Now all the others were round him too, astonished. Fatty? How had they missed him?

"You *are* a lot of donkeys," said Fatty, in his cheerful

14

voice. "I bet you met the train that comes in four minutes before mine. Buster was *much* more sensible! He knew enough to wait for the right one – and there he was, prancing round the platform, barking like mad when he saw me. I looked for you, but you were nowhere to be seen."

"Oh, Fatty – we must have met the wrong train – and we've made an *awful* mistake," said Daisy, troubled. "We thought you might be in disguise, just to play a joke on us – and when we couldn't see you anywhere, we followed a man we thought was you – and oh, Fatty, he asked us the way to some house or other – and we took him to yours!"

"Well!" said Fatty, and roared with laughter. "You are a lot of mutts. Where's this poor fellow? We'd better put him right."

The man was even now walking out of the gate, muttering and looking furious – as indeed he had every right to be. He stopped and looked at the name on the gate.

"Ha! You do not bring me to Grintriss. This is not Grintriss. You are wicket! You treat a sick man so!" He began to cough again.

The children were alarmed, and felt very sorry. However could they explain their mistake? He would never, never understand! He stalked up to them, blowing his nose with a trumpeting sound.

"Wicket! Wicket!" he repeated. "Very bad. Wicket!"

He began to shout at them in French, waving his arms about. They listened in dismay. Suppose Mrs. Trotteville came out? It would be even worse to explain their silly mistake to her than to this man.

A bell rang loudly and a bicycle stopped suddenly at the kerb. A very familiar voice hailed them.

"Now, then! What's all this?"

"Mr. Goon!" groaned Larry. "Old Clear-Orf. He would turn up, of course."

Buster danced round Mr. Goon in delight, barking furiously. Mr. Goon kept a watchful eye on him, thankful that he had on his thickest trousers.

"Nasty little yapping dog," he said. "Call him off or I'll give him a kick."

Fatty called Buster, and the Scottie came most reluctantly. Oh, for a bite at that big, loud-voiced policeman! Goon spoke to the bewildered Frenchman.

"What's all this? Have these children been annoying you? I'll report them, if so."

The man went off into a long and angry speech, but as it was all in French Mr. Goon didn't understand a word. He debated whether he should ask Fatty to translate for him – but how was he to trust that fat boy's translation? Fatty looked at Goon with a gleam in his eye.

"Don't you want to know what he's saying, Mr. Goon?" he said politely. "I can just catch a few words now and again. Er – he doesn't seem to like the look of you, I'm afraid. It sounds as if he's calling you names."

Mr. Goon felt out of his depth. These pests of children again – and this foreigner who appeared to be quite mad – and that nasty little dog longing to get at his ankles! Mr. Goon felt that the best and most dignified thing to do was to bicycle away immediately.

So, with a snort that sounded like "Gah" he pushed off from the kerb and sailed away down the road, followed by a fusillade of barks from the disappointed Buster.

"Thank goodness!" said Daisy, fervently, and all the five agreed.

It's Nice to be Together Again

The Frenchman stared after the policeman in surprise. In France policemen did not behave like that. They were interested and excited when a complaint was made to them, they listened, they took notes – but this policeman had said "Gah" and gone cycling away. Extraordinary!

He began to cough. Fatty felt sorry for him, and began to talk to him in perfect French. Trust old Fatty to know the right thing to do! The others stood round, listening in admiration. Really, Fatty might be French!

"How does he learn French like that?" wondered Daisy. "Nobody at our school could even *begin* to talk like that. Really, Fatty is a most surprising person."

The man began to calm down. He took a little notebook out of his pocket and opened it. "I will show you the name," he said. "Grintriss. Why should nobody know this Grintriss house?"

He showed Fatty something written down on a page of a notebook. The others peeped over his arm to look.

"Oh! GREEN-TREES!" said Daisy. "Why ever didn't you say so? You kept saying Grintriss."

"Yes. Grintriss," repeated the man, puzzled. "All the time I say 'Grintriss, pliss, where is zis house?' "

"It's Green-Trees," said Daisy, pronouncing it slowly and carefully.

"Grintriss," said the man, again. "And now – where is zis house? I ask of you for the last time."

He looked as if he were going to burst into tears. Fatty took his arm. "Come on. I'll show you. No tricks this time, we'll take you there."

And off they all went together, Fatty suddenly jabbering in French again. Down the road, round the corner, up the hill and into a quiet little lane. In the middle of it was a small and pretty house, smoke curling from its chimneys.

"Green-Trees," said Fatty, pointing to the name on the white gate.

"Ah – Grintriss," said the man, in delight and raised his hat to the two girls. "Mesdemoiselles, adieu! I go to find my sistair!"

17

He disappeared up the little front path. Bets gave a sigh and slipped her arm through Fatty's. "What a shame to welcome you home with a silly muddle like this, Fatty. We meant to be on the platform ready to give you a wonderful welcome – and only Buster was there – and we'd gone off after somebody who wasn't in the *least* like you."

"Yes – but that's the worst of Fatty when he puts on a disguise," grumbled Pip. "He never does look in the least like himself. Come on, Fatty – let's take you back home now. Your mother will be wondering what's become of you."

Mrs. Trotteville was quite relieved to see Fatty and the others trooping into the hall. She came out to greet them.

"Frederick! Did you miss your train? How late you are! Welcome home again."

"Hallo, Mother! What a nice smell from the kitchen! Smells like steak and onions. Buster, what do *you* think?"

"Wuff!" said Buster, ready to agree with every word that Fatty said. He dashed round Fatty's legs, galloped behind the couch, appeared again, and then threaded his way at top speed between all the chairs.

"Jet-propelled obstacle race," said Fatty. "Hey, Buster, look where you're going, you'll knock me over."

"He always behaves like that when you first come home," said Mrs. Trotteville. "I only hope he gets over the excitement soon. I simply daren't walk a step when he goes mad like this."

"He's a darling," said Bets. "I know how he feels when Fatty comes home. I feel rather the same myself."

Fatty gave her a sudden hug. "Well, don't *you* start racing round the furniture on all-fours," he said. "Tell me – any mysterious mysteries or insoluble problems cropped up this last week? What a shame you all got home before I did!"

"Nothing's turned up yet," said Pip. "But I bet something will now you're here. Adventures go to the adventurous, you know."

"I do hope nothing *does* turn up," said Mrs. Trotteville. "Or I shall have that silly Mr. Goon round here again. Now, the one *I* like is your friend, Superintendent Jenks!"

They all stared at her. "*Superintendent!* You don't mean that Chief-Inspector Jenks is a superintendent now!" said Larry. "My word – he's going up and up, isn't he?"

"We knew him first when he was an Inspector," said Bets, remembering. "And then he became a Chief-Inspector. Now he's a Superintendent. I'm glad. He's getting very very high-up, isn't he? I hope he'll still like to know us."

"I expect he will," said Mrs. Trotteville smiling. "Oh, dear – I do wish Cook would keep the kitchen door shut when she is doing onions – what a smell came in here then."

"Keep the door shut when it's steak and onions?" said Fatty, in horror. "*Shut*, did you say? Shut out a heavenly smell like that? Mother, don't you realise that I have, as usual, been half-starved all the term?"

"Well, it's a pity you weren't," said his mother, looking at his tight overcoat. "Those buttons look as if they are just about to burst off. Your trunk has come, Frederick. Do you want to unpack it, and get ready for lunch straight away? We're having it early as I thought you would be hungry."

"Mother, I do love you when you think things like that," said Fatty, in a sudden burst of affection. "I'm starving!"

"Cupboard love!" said his mother, amused at Fatty's sudden hug.

"Can all the others stay to lunch as well?" asked Fatty, hopefully.

"Yes, if you'd like to share your bit of steak and onions round," said his mother. But not even Fatty could rise to that, and so he said good-bye to the other four very reluctantly.

"They can all come to tea this afternoon, if you like," said Mrs. Trotteville. "I'll get in plenty of cakes. Frederick, do control Buster. He's gone mad again. It really makes me giddy to watch him."

"Buster! Behave yourself!" said Fatty, and the mad little Scottie turned himself miraculously into a quiet and peaceful little lamb, lying down on Fatty's feet and licking his shoes.

"Come back at three," said Fatty, and took the others to the front gate. "We'll have a good old talk and you can tell me all the news. So-long!" He went back to the house, sniffing for steak and onions again.

"I suppose, Frederick, you don't know anything about a bulky-looking foreigner who came to the front door this morning, and told Jane that this house was Grintriss, and wanted to force his way in and see some sister of his — do you?" said Mrs. Trotteville, when Fatty came back. "He kept talking about some 'wicket children' when Jane told him this wasn't the house. You hadn't anything to do with him, I suppose? You haven't been up to your tricks again already, I hope.'

"Of course not," said Fatty, looking quite hurt. "Poor fellow — I found him at the front gate, and we all took him to the place he wanted to go to. Green-Trees, down Holly Lane. Oh, Mother, there's that heavenly smell again. Do you mind if I go and smell it even nearer? I haven't seen Cook or Jane yet."

"Very well. But DON'T try lifting fried onions out of the pan," said Mrs. Trotteville. "Oh, Frederick — it's very nice to have you back — but I do wish I always knew what you were up to! Please don't get mixed up in anything alarming these holidays. Pip's mother was saying to me only yesterday that everything has been so *peaceful* this last week."

There was no answer. Fatty was already in the kitchen sampling half-fried strips of onion, while Cook and Jane

20

giggled at him, and promised to provide him with new gingerbread, hot scones and home-made raspberry jam when the others came to tea that afternoon. They loved Fatty.

"A caution, that's what he is," Cook told her friends. "Honestly, you just never know what's going to happen when Master Frederick is about."

Fatty enjoyed his lunch thoroughly, and told his mother all about his last term. He appeared, as always, to have done extremely well.

"Though there *may* be something on my report about the – er – the advisability of sticking to my own voice," he said, making his mother look up in surprise. "It's all right, Mother. It just means that my ventriloquism has been rather successful this term."

One of Fatty's talents was the ability to throw his voice, and he was now a very fine ventriloquist indeed – but unfortunately the masters at school did not approve of this as much as the boys did. Fatty's class had spent one whole morning searching for an apparently injured man somewhere up in the school attic. The groans had been tremendous and had caused a great sensation.

When it had been discovered that it was merely a ventriloquial stunt of Fatty's there had been another sensation – but not a very happy one for Fatty. In fact, he hadn't felt it wise to do any more ventriloquism that term, which was, he thought, a great pity. He would get out of practice!

At three o'clock exactly there was the tramp of feet going down the garden to Fatty's shed. Fatty saw Larry, Daisy, Pip and Bets passing by under his window and hurriedly stopped his unpacking.

He shot downstairs with Buster, and went to join the others in his big shed at the bottom of the garden.

This was playroom, store-room, changing-room – anything that Fatty wanted. He had a key for it, and kept it well and truly locked. There were too many disguises and odd clothes that he didn't want grown-ups to see. His mother would certainly have been astonished to see some of the old things he had picked up at jumble sales – dreadful old hats, ragged shawls, voluminous skirts, corduroy trousers, down-at-heel boots!

"Hallo!" said Fatty, appearing just as the others were looking in at the shed window to see if he was there. "I'll unlock the door. I slipped down just after dinner to light the oil-stove. It should be nice and warm now."

They all went in. It certainly was nice and warm. The sun slid in at one window and lighted up the inside of the shed. It looked dusty and untidy.

"I'll clean it up for you," promised Daisy, looking round. "I say – it's nice to meet like this again, isn't it – all the Five Find-Outers together!"

"With nothing to find out!" said Pip. "I like it best when we've got something exciting on hand. And remember, Fatty, we go back to school a whole week before you do, so there isn't a great deal of time to get going on something."

"We can always practise a bit," suggested Larry. "You know – go out in disguise – or do a spot of shadowing – or watching."

"Yes. We could do that," said Fatty. "I want to practise my ventriloquism too – I've got out of practice this last term."

"Oh, yes, *do* practise that!" begged Bets. "Let's make some plans."

"Right," said Fatty, obligingly. "We will!"

Many ridiculous plans were discussed that afternoon over a really super-tea. Cook had kept her word, and there were lashings of hot scones and raspberry jam, new and very sticky gingerbread with raisins in, and a big round chocolate cake with a special filling made by Cook

Buster had dog biscuits spread with potted meat, and approved of this very highly.

"It's three-treats-in-one for him," explained Fatty. "First he gets a fine sniff at the biscuits and potted meat. Then he gets a fine lick at them. Then he gets a wonderful crunch at them. Three-meals-in-one, so to speak."

"Wuff," said Buster, thumping his tail hard.

"And what is more," said Fatty, cutting himself a huge slice of the chocolate cake, "what is more, we can have every bit of this cake to ourselves. Potted-meat-biscuits take the *whole* of Buster's attention. He hasn't even *seen* this cake yet."

"And when he does, it won't be there," said Pip. "Not if I can help it, anyway."

They got back to their plans again. Fatty was in an uproarious mood, and made them all laugh till they choked.

"What about taking a clothes-horse with us, Larry, and going into the main street and pretending to be workmen chipping up the road?" suggested Fatty. "Just you and I, Larry. Pip's not big enough yet to pass as a workman. We could put the clothes-horse round us, like workman do, hang a red flag on it, and chip up the road!"

"Don't be an idiot," said Larry. "We'd get into an awful row."

"I bet old Goon would let us sit there all morning chipping up the road," said Fatty. "He'd never dream of asking us what we were doing."

"Fatty, I'm going to dare you to do something," said Daisy, with a sudden giggle. "Look – I'm trying to sell these tickets for our Church Sale. I dare you to try and sell one to old Goon."

"Easy!" said Fatty. "Very easy! Give me one. I'll sell it tomorrow. That shall be my little task."

"What shall *I* do?" asked Larry.

"Er – let me see – yes, what about you putting on overalls, taking a pail and a leather and going to clean somebody's windows?" said Fatty.

"Oh, no!" said Larry, in alarm. "Nothing like that!"

"Yes, do, do!" begged Daisy and Bets.

"Only you'll have to choose a house that is all on one floor – a bungalow, for instance," said Pip. "You won't need a ladder then – and there wouldn't be so many windows to clean! Larry as window-cleaner! That's good!"

"Do I have to *ask* if I can clean the windows?" said Larry, looking desperate. "I mean – I can't just go to a house and start cleaning, can I? They might have their own regular window-cleaner."

"Yes, that's true. You must ask first," said Fatty, solemnly. "And if you get any payment, you can buy one of Daisy's Sale tickets."

"Oh, I say! said Larry. "That's a bit hard." It occurred to him that these sudden plans were rather a mistake!

"What shall *I* do?" said Pip, with a giggle. They all looked at him. "You can shadow Goon sometime tomorrow," said Fatty firmly. "Shadow him so that he doesn't know you're following him – do it really properly."

"All right," said Pip. "I can do that, I think. What about the girls?"

"We'll think of something for them to do when we've done our tasks," said Fatty. "Now, any one want this last

24

bit of gingerbread – or shall I cut it into five?"

It was duly cut into five. "Any one seen Superintendent Jenks these hols?" asked Fatty, handing round the gingerbread. "Jolly good that he's promoted again, isn't it?"

"Super!" said Bets.

"Yes – super – intendent," said Pip, and everyone punched him. "No – none of us has seen him – we're not likely to see him either, unless we have something in the mystery line to solve."

"I wish he'd hand us over a few of his cases," said Fatty, stacking the plates together. "I'm sure we could help. I mean – we've had a good bit of experience now, haven't we?"

"The only thing is, Goon always knows about the cases, too, and he does get in our way when we're both working on the same mystery," said Daisy. "I wish we could work on some more clues – and suspects – and all the rest. It *is* such fun!"

They got out some cards and began to play a game. It was nice to be all together again. Things weren't the same somehow without Fatty. He said and did such ridiculous things, and nobody ever knew what he would do next.

Pip looked at his watch after a time and sighed. "I must go," he said. "Come on, Bets. We shall only get into a row if we're late. Why does time always go so fast when you don't want it to?"

"Don't forget, Pip and Larry, you've got jobs to do tomorrow," said Fatty, slipping the cards back into their case. "Report here tomorrow after tea – and I'll have the money for Goon's ticket ready for you, Daisy!"

She laughed. "It will be more difficult than you think!" she said. "Come on, Larry."

As Fatty cleared up the shed when the others had gone, he wondered how he could get Mr. Goon to buy the ticket. He ran his eye over the clothes hanging up at one side of

25

the shed. He must certainly disguise himself, for Goon would never, never buy a ticket from him if he went as himself!

"I'll go as an old woman, and pretend to read his hand!" thought Fatty. "He believes in that sort of nonsense. It should be fun!"

Pip was also planning his own task. When should he shadow Mr. Goon? Of course, it would be easiest to do it in the dark; but he didn't know what time Goon went out at night, and he couldn't very well hang about outside his house for hours. No, it would have to be in the morning, when Goon went out on his bicycle. Pip would take his and follow him. He would pretend that Goon was a suspect — a burglar or a thief — and track him wherever he went!

So, next morning, Pip got his bicycle and set out to the street where the policeman lived. There was his house, with POLICE above it in big letters. Pip got off his bicycle, propped it against a big tree, and then quietly let all the air out of one tyre.

Now he could mess about with the wheel, pretending to pump up his tyre, and nobody would bother about why he was there, even if he had to wait for half an hour or more.

He did have to wait a good time, and got rather tired of pumping up his tyre and letting the air out again. But at last Mr. Goon appeared, wheeling his bicycle out, his trousers neatly clipped in at the ankles.

Pip was surprised to see a skinny little boy of about eleven following Goon to the door. Goon shouted a few words to him, mounted his bicycle ponderously and rode off up the street. Pip slid on to his saddle and rode off too.

Goon didn't seem to have the slightest idea that he was being followed. He sailed along, waving to this person and that in a very condescending manner. He got off at the front gate of a house, propped his bicycle up against the fence and went to the front door. Pip waited beside a hedge.

Out came Goon again, and rode down the road and into the main street. He got off at the post-office and went inside. Pip got tired of waiting for him and thought longingly of ice-creams. He was just near a shop that sold them. He suddenly decided to nip in and get one.

But, while he nipped in and got one, Mr. Goon came out and sailed away again on his bicycle. Pip only *just* managed to spot him, crammed his ice-cream down his throat so that he almost froze himself, and raced after Goon.

On the way he passed Mrs. Trotteville, Fatty's mother. She had Buster with her, and as soon as he saw Pip, and heard his voice calling out "good morning", he left Mrs. Trotteville and raced after Pip.

"No, Buster. Not this morning. Go back, there's a good dog!" shouted Pip. But Buster laboured after him, panting. Fatty had gone out without him – so he would go with Pip. But Buster couldn't keep up with Pip on his bicycle and was soon left behind. He followed at a distance, still panting.

Mr. Goon had gone down a lane that led nowhere except to a farm. Pip just managed to see him disappearing round the corner. He guessed what he had gone to the farm for. The farmer had been complaining bitterly that his sheep had been worried by dogs. Goon must have gone to get details of the dogs. Oh, well – Pip could sit under a hedge and wait for Goon to come out again. It was a bit dull shadowing him, really. He wondered how Larry was getting on with his window-cleaning.

Pip got off his bicycle, hid it in a ditch and then crept through a gap into the field. Sheep were there, with some fat woolly lambs about three months old. They were skipping about in a ridiculous fashion.

Pip sat with his back against a hawthorn tree and watched them. Suddenly he heard the scampering of feet and loud panting breath – and in another second Buster had

27

flung himself on him through the gap in the hedge! He licked Pip's face and yelped for joy. "Found you!" he seemed to say. "Found you!"

"Oh, Buster!" said Pip. "Stop licking me!" He pushed Buster away, and the dog ran out into the field in a wide circle, barking. Some near-by lambs started away in alarm and ran to their mother-sheep.

And then a loud familiar voice came through the hedge. "Ho! So it's that fat boy's dog that chases Farmer Meadows' sheep, is it? I might have guessed it. I'll catch that dog and have him shot. I've just this minute been to the farm to get particulars of sheep-chasing dogs — and here I've got one caught in the act!"

Mr. Goon came crashing through the hedge, and Pip at once sprang to his feet. "Buster wasn't chasing the sheep!" he cried, indignantly. "He came to find *me*. He's only arrived this very minute."

"I'll catch that dog and take him off with me," said Mr. Goon, simply delighted to think that he could find such a good reason for catching Buster.

But it wasn't so easy to catch the Scottie. In fact, it was far easier for Buster to catch Mr. Goon, as the policeman soon realised when Buster kept running at him and then backing away. In the end he had to shout to Pip to call him off. Pip called him — and Goon just had time to mount his bicycle and pedal away at top speed!

"I wonder where Fatty is," groaned Pip. "I must find him and tell him about this. Blow you, Buster! — what did you want to follow me for? NOW you're in for trouble!"

Pip got on his bicycle and rode off. Buster ran beside him, keeping a good look-out for Mr. Goon. He would have very much liked another pounce at his ankles — but Goon was out of sight, on his way home. Visions of a nice hot cup of coffee, well-sugared, and a slice of home-made cake floated in his mind.

Pip rode to Fatty's house, but he wasn't there. "Blow!" said Pip. "I suppose he's gone off to sell his ticket to Goon. I wish I'd seen him. I bet he looks exactly like some old woman shopping in the town!"

Fatty had had a most enjoyable time in his shed choosing a disguise to wear when he went to sell the ticket to Mr. Goon. He had chosen a rather long black skirt, a black jumper, a shapeless dark-red coat and a hat he had bought at the last jumble sale.

It was black straw, and had a few dark-red roses in the front. Fatty put on a wig of dark hair, and made up his face, putting in a few artful wrinkles here and there.

He looked at himself in the mirror and grinned. Then he frowned — and immediately the face of a cross old woman looked back at him out of the mirror!

"I wish the others could see me," thought Fatty. "They'd hoot with laughter. Now, where's my hand-bag?"

The hand-bag was a very old one of his mother's. In it was a powder-compact, a handkerchief and a few hair-pins, all of which Fatty kept there for use when he disguised himself as a woman. He delighted in taking out the powder case and dabbing powder on his nose, as he had so often seen women do! His mother would have been most astonished to see him.

He unlocked the door of his shed, and opened it a little, listening. Was any one about? Or could he slip safely out into the road?

He could hear nothing, so he slipped out of the shed, locked the door and made his way up the side-path through the shrubbery.

As he went through the bushes, a voice hailed him. "Hey, you! What you doing there!"

It was the gardener, looking with interest at the shabby old woman.

Fatty immediately went all foreign. He flapped about with his hands, moved his shoulders up and down and said "Ackle-eeta-oomi-poggy-wo?"

"Can't you speak English?" said the gardener. "See — there's the kitchen door if you want anything."

"Tipply-opply-erica-coo," said Fatty in a most grateful voice, and slid out of the gardener's sight. He grinned to himself. His disguise must be pretty good if the gardener didn't see through it!

He decided that it would be quite a good idea to go on being rather foreign. It was so easy to talk gibberish! Fatty could go on and on for a very long time, apparently speaking in a foreign language, shrugging his shoulders like his French master at school, and waggling his hands about.

He made his way down the road. Nobody took the least notice of him, which was very good. Fatty decided that he looked rather like one of the faded old women who sometimes sat on committees with his mother.

He came to the road where Goon lived and went up to his house. Was Goon in? Fatty knocked at the door.

It opened, and a skinny little boy stood there, the same skinny little fellow who had followed Goon to the door when Pip had been waiting for him.

The boy looked at him with sharp eyes. "Mr. Goon's out," he said. "There's only my Mum in. She's cleaning. If

30

you want to leave a message I'll call her."

"Ah – zat would be kind," said Fatty, giving the boy a sudden beaming smile. "I vill come in."

He pushed past the boy and went into Goon's office. He sat down, spreading out his skirts and patting the back of his hair with his hand.

"I'll fetch me Mum," said the boy, who didn't quite know what to make of this visitor. Was she a friend of Mr. Goon?

" 'Ere, Mum – there's a funny old foreign lady come to see Mr. Goon," Fatty heard the boy say. "She's set herself down in the office."

"All right. I'll see what she wants," said Mum's voice. Mum then appeared at the office-door, wiping her hands on an apron.

Fatty gave her a gracious smile and nodded her head. "I come to see dear Mr. Goon," he announced. "He is expecting me – yes?"

"I don't rightly know," said Mum. "He's out just now. Will you wait? I'm just cleaning out for him – I come every morning. I have to bring Bert with me because it's holidays, but he's useful."

Fatty beamed at the skinny little woman, who really looked very like Bert. "Ikkle-dokka-runi-pie," he said, in a very earnest voice.

"Pardon?" said Mum, startled. "You're foreign, aren't you? I had a foreigner once who lodged with me. She was right down clever – read my hand like a book!"

"Ah – so!" said Fatty. "I too read the hand. Like a book."

"Do you really?" said Mum, and came a little farther into the room. Fatty racked his brains to remember who she was. He knew he had seen her before. Then he remembered. Of course – she was a friend of Jane, the house parlour-maid, and sometimes came to help Cook when

31

.they had a party — he had heard them talking about her — what was her name now? Ah, yes—Mickle.

Mum wiped her hands again on her apron and held one out to Fatty. "What's my hand tell you?" she asked, eagerly.

Fatty took it in his and frowned over it. "Ah — your name it is Mickle! Mrs. Mickle. You live at — at — Shepherd's Crescent. . . ."

"Coo!" said Mum, most impressed. "Is that all written in my hand? Go on."

"You have five sisters," said Fatty, remembering the gossip he had heard. "And er — er — you have brothers — how many? It is difficult to see in your hand."

"I've got six," said Mum, helpfully. "Perhaps they're hidden under that bit of dirt there. I'd have washed me hands if I'd known you were coming."

"I see illnesses here," went on Fatty, "and children — and cups and cups of tea — and . . ."

"That's right!" broke in Mum, quite excited. "I've bin ill many a time — and I've got five children — Bert there is the youngest — and the cups of tea I've had — well, I must have had thousands in me life!"

"Millions," said Fatty, still bent over her hand.

"Fancy you even seeing them cups of tea there," said Mum. She raised her voice. "Bert! This lady's a real wonder at reading hands. You come and listen."

Bert was already listening just outside the door. He came right in when his mother called. He looked at Fatty disbelievingly.

"Where do you see them cups of tea?" he asked. "How do you know they're not cups of coffee?"

Fatty decided that he didn't much like Bert. He thought it would be very nice indeed to read Bert's hand and see a great many spankings there. But Bert didn't ask to have his hand read. He kept them both firmly behind his back

32

as if afraid that Fatty would start reading them at once. Young Bert already had quite a lot of things in his life that he didn't want any one to know about!

Someone rode up to the front gate and got off a bicycle. "Coo – here's Mr. Goon back already and I haven't got the kettle on for his coffee!" said Mum, and disappeared at once. Mr. Goon opened the front door and came heavily into the hall. Mum called out to him.

"Mr. Goon, sir! There's a lady wanting to see you. I've put her in the office."

Mr. Goon went into the kitchen. "Who is she?" Fatty heard him say. "What's she come for?"

"I didn't make so bold as to ask her *that*," said Mum, putting a kettle on the stove. "She's a foreigner by the sound of her – funny-looking, you know, and speaks queer."

"She read Mum's hand," said Bert, slyly.

"You hold your tongue, young Bert," said Mum, sharply. "She read it like a book, sir – knew me name and everything. One of these clever ones. You ready for your cup of coffee, sir?"

"Yes. I could do with one," said Goon. "I've been attacked by a dog this morning."

"You don't say!" said Mum. "Did he bite you?"

Mr. Goon liked sympathy. He enlarged quite a bit on Buster's light-hearted game with him.

"It's a wonder my trousers aren't torn to bits," he said. "The dog came at me time and again. If I wasn't pretty nippy, I'd have been bitten more than I was. Good thing I had my thickest trousers on."

"Well, there now! What a thing to happen to you, Mr. Goon!" said Mum. Bert stared down at Mr. Goon's trousers to see if they were torn. They didn't appear to be.

"You going to report the dog?" asked Bert.

"I caught it chasing sheep," said Goon, taking off his

33

helmet. "Very serious crime, that, for a dog. I tried to catch it, but I couldn't. I'd give anything to have that dog here under lock and key. I'd teach it a few things!"

"What would you give me if I got it for you?" asked Bert. Goon stared at him. Mum was taking no notice; she was busy at the cupboard with a cake-tin. Goon nodded his head towards the hall, and Bert followed him there.

Fatty had heard every word. He wondered whose dog this was that Goon was talking about. He knew that the farmer had been worried by sheep-chasing dogs. It never occurred to him that Goon was actually talking about Buster.

A whispered conversation followed. Fatty only caught a few words, but he guessed the rest. Goon was arranging with young Bert to catch the dog and bring it to him. The sum of half a crown was mentioned. Fatty frowned. How wrong of Goon to do a thing like that! He wished he knew whose dog it was –he would certainly warn the owner!

Goon appeared in the office, looking rather pleased with himself, and young Bert went back to the kitchen.

Fatty didn't get up. He held out a gracious hand and bowed in a very lady-like way. Goon was rather impressed with this behaviour, though not with Fatty's clothes. Still –foreigners did seem to wear peculiar things sometimes.

"What can I do for you, Madam?" said Goon.

"I am a friend of Mrs. Trotteville," said Fatty, truthfully. "A vairy GREAT friend."

"Ah," said Goon, impressed. He was in awe of Mrs. Trotteville. "You staying with her, then?"

"I shall be wiz her for three wiks," said Fatty, sticking to the truth. "I sell tickets for the beeg Sale. You will buy one, yes?"

"Er – well – can I offer you a cup of coffee?" said Goon, seeing Mum coming in with a tray. "I hear you can read hands. I suppose you'll be doing that at the Sale?"

"You would like me to read your beeg, beeg hand now – and you will buy a ticket?" offered Fatty.

Mr. Goon couldn't resist having his hand read. Mum fetched another cup of coffee – and Mr. Goon held out a large hand, palm upwards, to Fatty. How Fatty wished that Larry and the others could see him!

A Few Reports

That evening, after tea, the Five Find-Outers met in Fatty's shed as arranged. Fatty was there first, grinning whenever he remembered how he had read Goon's hand. In his pocket were two half-crowns that Goon had given him for Daisy's ticket. Easy!

The others all arrived together. Fatty welcomed them. He had orangeade and biscuits, which everyone was pleased to see, in spite of the fact that they had all made a very good tea not half an hour before.

"Now, are we all ready? We'll have our various reports," said Fatty. "You first, Pip – you seem to be bursting with news."

"I am," said Pip, and poured out the story of how he had shadowed Goon, seen him go to the farmhouse, and waited for him in the field. He told how Buster had also shadowed *him*, and burst on him as he sat watching the sheep and the lambs.

"Then old Buster got excited and some lambs were afraid and scampered away, making the sheep run," said Pip. "Up came old Goon and said that Buster ought to be shot for worrying sheep!"

"Good gracious!" said Daisy. "Surely he didn't mean that? Buster has never, never chased a sheep, has he, Fatty?"

"Never," said Fatty, who was listening intently. "Go on, Pip."

"There's nothing much more to tell except that Goon was idiot enough to try and catch Buster," said Pip. "And Buster had a fine old game with him, of course, trying to nip his ankles. It would have served Goon right if he *had* nipped them! The only reason that Goon said that Buster was chasing sheep was just so that he could report him — but, oh, Fatty, Buster *couldn't* be shot just on Goon's report, could he?"

"Don't worry. I'll see that he isn't," said Fatty, grimly. "We'd get on to Chief-Inspector — I mean, Superintendent — Jenks at once! It's funny, though, when I went to see Goon this morning, he came in talking all about some dog or other that he wanted brought in for sheep-chasing — I bet it was Buster, though he didn't say the name."

"But — why did he tell you?" said Pip, surprised. "He might have guessed you'd hear about it from me."

"Oh, he didn't know *I* was sitting there in his office," said Fatty. "I was disguised, of course. I'll have to think about this story of yours, Pip. I have an idea that Goon has made some arrangement with a nasty, skinny little kid to catch Buster. Son of a woman who was cleaning the house for Goon."

"I saw him at the door," said Pip, remembering. "Gosh, he'd never have the nerve to catch Buster, surely?"

"I don't know. We'll have to watch out," said Fatty. "Listen and I'll tell you how I sold the ticket to Goon."

Daisy gave a shriek of delight. "Oh, did you really manage to? Oh, Fatty, you *are* clever! You must have been jolly well disguised."

"Well — I was," said Fatty, trying to be modest. "As a matter of fact, I don't believe even Bets here would have guessed it was me. I went as a friend of my mother, a foreign one, rather down-at-heel — you know, old lady-

36

gone-to-seed-a-bit! Staying with dear Mrs. Trotteville for three weeks."

Every one roared. "Oh, Fatty!" said Bets. "It's so true too – you are a friend of your mother – and you *are* here for three weeks. Marvellous!"

"I sold the ticket by reading Goon's hand," went on Fatty, enjoying himself. "He stuck his great fat paw on my knee, and I exclaimed over it, and said how extraordinary it was – and so it was, with its enormous fingers and great fat palm. I could hardly see the lines on it for fat."

"What did you tell him?" asked Daisy.

"Oh – I told him his name was Theophilus, and that he had plenty of nephews – one very clever one called Ern," said Fatty. Everyone laughed. Mr. Goon disliked Ern intensely. "I told him he would handle a lot of money," went on Fatty.

"Yes! His wages every week!" grinned Pip.

"But the best bit was where I looked hard at his hand – like this," said Fatty, clutching Daisy's hand suddenly and making her jump. He peered closely at it, then held it away, then peered at it again.

"Ha! Zis is a vairy pee-culiar thing I see!" said Fatty, sounding like the Frenchwoman again. "I see – a fat boy – a beeg fat boy."

There were roars of laughter at this. "Oh, Fatty!" said Bets. "You pretended you saw yourself in Goon's hand! What did he say?"

"He seemed very startled," said Fatty, in his own voice. "He said. 'What! That toad! Tell me more.'"

"So you told him more?" said Larry, grinning.

"Oh, yes. I said 'BEWAAAAARE of zis fat boy. There is some mystery here. Ze fat boy and the mystery are to-gezzer!'" Fatty paused and twinkled round at the others.

"That made Goon sit up, I can tell you. He said, 'What!

37

A mystery! Go on – tell me about it. What mystery is it?' "

"What did you say?" said Bets, with a sudden giggle.

"I said, 'I do not know zis mystery. It will come. But BEWAAAAARE of zis beeg, fat boy!' "

"Oh, Fatty! I do wish I'd been there," said Bets, and the others all agreed fervently. Oh, to have sat and watched Fatty reading Mr. Goon's hand!

"Is that all?" asked Daisy. "Tell us it all over again."

"No. Not now," said Fatty, reluctantly. "We ought to hear Larry's story. Time's getting on. Anyway, the result of all this amazing hand-reading was that Goon handed over two half-crowns for Daisy's ticket like an absolute lamb. He even said that if I was going to be at the Sale he'd be along for another hand-reading to see if the mystery was any nearer. He simply BEAMED at me!"

"Oh, dear – what a wonderful morning you had," said Larry, as Fatty handed over two half-crowns to the delighted Daisy. "Now I'll tell my story."

"Yes, tell yours," said Daisy. "You should have seen him dressed up as a window-cleaner, Fatty! He borrowed an old pair of dirty blue dungarees, put on a frightful old cloth cap that has hung in the shed for ages, and made himself filthy – hands, face and neck! HONESTLY, I'd never employ him as a window-cleaner. He looked more like a sweep."

Fatty grinned. "Good work," he said to Larry. "Go on – tell us what you did."

"Well," said Larry, "I dressed up, just as Daisy's told you. And I took an old pail and a leather, and off I went."

"Where did you go?" asked Fatty.

"Well, I remembered I'd better not choose a house that needed a ladder for upstairs windows," said Larry. "So I tried to think of a bungalow somewhere, with the windows all on the one floor. And I remembered seeing one next to that house called Green-Trees – do you remember, the one that that foreigner went to — the man we mistook to be Fatty."

"Oh, yes, I remember the bungalow too," said Fatty. "Good for you! In Holly Lane, wasn't it? A little place with an untidy garden, standing a bit back from the road."

"That's right. What a memory you've got, Fatty! You never miss anything," said Larry. "Well, I took my pail and my leather and walked up the path to the bungalow. I knocked at the door."

"Was anyone in?" asked Bets.

"I didn't think so at first, because nobody answered," said Larry. "So I knocked again, very loudly. And a voice said 'Come in.' I opened the door and yelled inside. 'Window-cleaner! Is it all right to do the windows now?' And somebody shouted 'Yes!' "

"Who was it? Did you see?" asked Fatty.

"No, I didn't," said Larry. "Anyway, I got some water from a water-butt outside, and started on the back windows — two of them. There wasn't any one in the room there; it was a bedroom with a single bed, a chair, and a table — rather poor. As I was doing these windows I heard the front door slam and somebody went up the path to the road. I didn't see him — or her, it might have been."

"Was the house left empty then?" asked Fatty.

"I thought so, at first. But when I came round to the front to do the front windows, I saw there was someone inside that room," said Larry. "And this is the queer part of my story."

Everyone sat up at once.

"Queer — how do you mean?" asked Fatty.

"Well, at first I thought there wasn't anyone in the room," said Larry, "and I thought I'd buck up and clean the windows and go, glad to have finished the job — actually, when I was doing it, I thought it was a bit silly! And then I suddenly saw someone on the floor."

"On the *floor*! Hurt, do you mean?" asked Pip.

"No. He didn't seem to be hurt," said Larry. "He seemed to be feeling the chairs — he felt first one, and then another, muttering to himself all the time."

"But what for?" asked Fatty. "And who was he, any-way?"

"I don't know. He looked a very *old* man," said Larry. "He had a kind of night-cap on his head, and he wore pyjamas and a dressing-gown. He kept feeling one chair after another — underneath them — and then he came to a chair that seemed to satisfy him. He nodded and gave a chuckle."

"Extraordinary! What did he do next?" asked Fatty, most interested.

"He crawled over the floor to a kind of wheel-chair, and somehow got into it," said Larry. "His night-cap slipped off and he was quite bald, poor old fellow. He sat in front of some kind of stove, and then he dropped off to sleep as I watched him."

"Didn't he see you looking in?" asked Bets.

"No. I think he's almost blind," said Larry. "He had to *feel* for the chairs — as if he couldn't really see them. Funny, wasn't it?"

"Yes. Very queer," said Pip. "I wonder what he was feeling all over the chairs for. Do you suppose he had got something hidden in one of them? Money, perhaps?"

"Possibly. He might be afraid of robbers and have hid-den his little hoard somewhere odd that he considered safe," said Fatty. "Well, it's a peculiar story, Larry, and it's a good thing you weren't a real window-cleaner — a dishonest one might easily have guessed what the old man was doing! Making sure his savings were still safe!"

"I stripped off my dungarees in the bushes, cleaned my-self up a bit with the leather, and went home," said Larry. "I'd really rather work on a *real* mystery than do all this pretend shadowing and disguising and window-cleaning. It doesn't really *lead* to anything!"

But Larry was wrong. Quite wrong. It led to quite a lot of things. It led, in fact, to a really first-class Mystery!

Where is Buster?

For the next day or two Fatty kept a sharp eye on Buster, wondering if the skinny little boy would really try to kidnap him. But there seemed to be no sign of Bert.

And then one evening Buster disappeared! Fatty had gone out on his bicycle with the others to the cinema, and had left Buster safely in the kitchen with the Cook, who was very fond of him. When he came back, he sat down and finished a book he was reading, and it wasn't until he had finished it that he realised that Buster had not come scampering to be with him as usual.

He went to the door and shouted. "Buster! Where are you?"

It was half-past ten. Cook and Jane had gone to bed. His mother and father were out playing bridge and the house was very quiet.

"BUSTER! Where are you?" yelled Fatty again.

A voice came from upstairs. "Oh, Master Frederick, is that you shouting? You did give me a start! Isn't Buster with you? He wanted to go out at half-past nine, and we thought he heard you coming in to put your bicycle away, so we let him out. Didn't you see him?"

"No, Jane! I haven't seen him since I've been in," said Fatty. "Where on earth can he be? I'll open the front door and yell."

He stood at the front door and shouted. "Buster! BUSTER!"

But no Buster came. Fatty was puzzled. Where could he have gone? Well, perhaps he would come in when his mother and father came back.

But Buster didn't. It was a very worried Fatty who greeted his parents when they came in at twelve o'clock.

"Frederick! Why aren't you in bed?" began his mother. "It's midnight!"

"Have you seen Buster?" said Fatty.... "You haven't? Gosh, then, where can he be?"

"He's probably gone to visit one of his friends and forgotten the time, like you do sometimes!" said his father. "Get to bed now. Buster will be back in the morning, barking outside at six o'clock and waking us all."

There was nothing for it but to go to bed. Fatty undressed and got between the sheets. But he couldn't help remembering the whispered conversation he had heard in Goon's little hall – and Bert's mean little face. Had Bert somehow got hold of Buster?

Buster didn't come barking at the front door in the morning. He hadn't even appeared by breakfast-time! Fatty was by now quite certain that somehow or other the skinny little boy had managed to get hold of the little Scottie. He went out into the garden to investigate. Perhaps he could find something to explain Buster's disappearance.

He did find something. He found a small bit of liver attached to a short piece of string. Fatty pounced on it, frowning fiercely.

"That's it! That little beast Bert must have come along with some liver, tied it on a bit of string and drawn it along for Buster to follow him. And old Buster leapt at it and got the liver and chewed the string in half. Then he must have followed Bert – and probably more liver – till Bert managed to slip a lead on him and take him off."

He threw the bit of liver away and went indoors angrily. The telephone bell rang as he walked into the hall. His father was there and took up the receiver.

"Hallo! Yes, this is Mr. Trotteville speaking. Who's that? Mr. Goon? What's that? Do speak up, please, I can only hear a mumble."

There was a short silence. Fatty stood nearby, listening. Mr. Goon! Now what was this?

"I can't believe it!" said Mr. Trotteville into the telephone. "Buster has never chased a thing in his life – except your ankles. All right – come and see me. I don't believe it!"

He put the receiver down and faced Fatty. "That fellow Goon says your dog Buster was caught red-handed last night, chasing sheep."

"It couldn't have been Buster," said Fatty. "It must be some other dog."

"He says he's got Buster in his shed now," said Mr. Trotteville. "He'll be shot, you know, if this is true. Where was he last night?"

"Someone came and enticed him away," said Fatty. "Someone who's told a lie about Buster! Who says they saw him chasing sheep?"

"A boy called Bert Mickle," said his father. "Goon says this boy was out walking in the fields last night, and actually saw Buster worrying the sheep. He managed to catch him, and slipped a rope under his collar. He took him to Mr. Goon's, but the policeman was out, so the boy locked the dog into the shed there – and he's there still. Now what are we to do?"

"It's an absolute untruth," said Fatty, looking rather white. "It's a plan laid between them. I'll pay Goon out for this. When's he coming, Dad?"

"In half an hour's time," said Mr. Trotteville. "I'll have to see him. I can't bear the sight of him."

Fatty disappeared. He knew quite certainly that Buster had not been chasing sheep. He also knew that the horrid

43

little Bert had told a lot of lies, and he was sure that Goon knew it And Buster might be shot because of all that!

Fatty raced down to his shed. He put on a red wig, inserted some false plastic teeth in front of his own and dressed himself in an old suit, with a butcher-boy's blue-and-white apron in front. Then he jumped on his bicycle and rode off down to Goon's house. He stood whistling on the pavement opposite, apparently reading a comic with great interest – but all the time he was watching for Goon to come out.

Goon came at last and wheeled his bicycle out of the front gate. He looked exceedingly pleased with himself, and hummed a little tune as he rode off.

The butcher-boy opposite scowled and folded up his comic. Leaving his bicycle beside the kerb, he crossed the road and went round to the back of Goon's house.

He glanced at the shed in the garden. A subdued but angry barking came from it. Then a scraping at the door. Fatty bit his lip. That was Buster all right!

He knocked at the back door. Mrs. Mickle came, wiping her hands on her apron as usual.

"You're wanted up at home, Mrs. Mickle," said Fatty. "Message to say you're to go at once."

"Oh, dear! oh, dear! I hope my mother's not been taken ill again," said Mrs. Mickle. "Bert! I'm wanted up at home. You'd better keep on here till I come back. Mr. Goon's out."

"Bert had better go with you," said Fatty, firmly. He wanted them both out of the way as quickly as possible.

"No. I'm staying here," said Bert, thinking of the tarts and buns he could take out of the larder with both Mr. Goon and his mother out of the house.

That was that. Bert was not going to move, Fatty could see. All right – he would make him!

Mrs. Mickle took off her apron and fled up the street.

Bert stood at the front door and watched her go. Fatty nipped in at the back door and hid himself in a cupboard outside the kitchen.

Bert came back, having shut the hall-door. He whistled. Ha, now for the larder! Fatty heard him go into the kitchen and open the larder door. It creaked. Fatty peeped out of the cupboard.

A hollow voice suddenly spoke behind Bert. "Beware! Your sins will find you out. BEWARE!"

Bert turned round in a hurry. There was nobody in the kitchen at all. He stood there, trembling, a small jam-tart in one hand.

"Who took that dog away last night?" said another voice, which seemed to come from behind the kitchen door. "Who took him away?"

"Don't, don't!" cried poor Bert, and the jam-tart fell from his hand. "I took him, I took him! Who is talking to me?"

A loud growling came from another corner and Bert yelled. He looked round for the dog but couldn't see one. Then a loud me-owing began. "MEEE-ow! MEEE-ow!"

But no cat was to be seen. Bert began to howl and tears poured down his cheeks. "Mum!" he cried. "Mum!"

But Mum was far away up the street. Fatty began again. "Who told a lie? Who took that dog away?"

"I'll tell the truth, I will, I will!" sobbed Bert. "I'm a bad boy, I am."

"BEWARE!" said the deep hollow voice again. It was too much for Bert. He fled into the hall and out of the front door, leaving it open as he went. Fatty heard the scampering of his feet, and grinned. So much for Bert. Served him right – trying to get an innocent dog shot!

Fatty went to the garden shed. He had with him a bunch of keys that he had seen hanging from a hook on the kitchen dresser. One of them unlocked the shed.

45

Buster flew at him, barking in delight. He careered round Fatty, and Fatty picked him up and squeezed him till the little Scottie had no breath left in his body. He licked Fatty's face vigorously.

Then Fatty suddenly caught sight of something — Mr. Goon's enormous black cat sitting high up on a wall, watching Buster out of sleepy insolent eyes. He knew he was too high up for any dog to catch. An idea came to Fatty.

"Just half a minute, Buster old fellow," he said, and put the Scottie inside the house, shutting the kitchen door on him.

Then he went to the great tom-cat. He stroked it and murmured flattering things into its pricked-up ears. It purred loudly. Most animals loved Fatty!

It allowed him to lift it off the wall and fondle it. He walked with it to the shed and took it inside. He set it down on a sack that had evidently been placed there for Buster, and stroked it.

Then he went swiftly to the door, shut it, locked it and took the keys back to the kitchen. Buster had been frantically scraping at the door, trying to get to Fatty. Fatty picked him up, and went out of Goon's house, across the road to his bicycle. He put Buster in the basket, and rode off whistling shrilly like an errand-boy, thinking happy thoughts!

"All right, Mr. Goon! You can take my father down to see Buster in the shed — threaten to have him shot! You'll find nothing there but your own black tom-cat!" Fatty grinned at his thoughts, and Buster yapped happily in the basket. Why had he been shut up like that? He didn't know. But nothing mattered now. He was with Fatty, and Buster's world was cheerful and happy once more.

Fatty shot in at his side-gate and cycled down to his shed. He tore off his errand-boy things. Then he shut Buster up in the shed, with many apologies, and went back to the house. Was Mr. Goon still there? Well, he could say what he liked! Buster was safe!

Mr. Goon Gets a Shock

Mr. Goon had been at Fatty's house for about five minutes, and was thoroughly enjoying himself. He knew that neither Mr. nor Mrs. Trotteville liked him, and it was pleasant to Mr. Goon to bring them such bad news about Buster.

Fatty sauntered into the room, and Mr. Goon looked at him triumphantly. "Morning, Mr. Goon," said Fatty. "Lovely April day, isn't it? Got any mystery in the offing yet?"

"I've come about that there dog of yours," said Mr. Goon, almost joyfully. "Been caught chasing sheep again."

"Rubbish," said Fatty, briskly. "Never chased one in his life!"

"I've got evidence," said Goon, going slightly purple. "And I've got the dog too, see? Locked up in my shed."

"I don't believe it," said Fatty. "I'll have to see the dog first, before I believe it's old Buster. He's not the dog in your shed, I'll be bound."

Mr. Trotteville looked at Fatty in surprise. Fatty winked at him. His father heaved a sigh of relief. He had no idea what Fatty was up to; but he began to feel that somehow, somewhere, Goon was not going to get away with this tale about Buster.

Goon went very purple indeed. He turned to Mr. Trotteville. "If you'll be so good, sir, as to come along with me and identify the dog, it would be a great help," he said. "Master Frederick had better come too. After all, it's his dog."

47

"I'll come all right," said Fatty. "You coming too, Dad?"

"Yes. I'll get the car out," said his father, still puzzled over Fatty's attitude. "You can come with me, Frederick. You cycle off, Goon, and we'll be there as soon as you are."

Mr. Trotteville went to get the car. Goon disappeared on his bicycle, purple but still triumphant. Fatty went to the telephone.

"Oh – is that Mrs. Hilton? Good morning. Please may I speak to Pip? Shan't keep him a minute."

Pip was fetched. Fatty spoke to him urgently. "Pip? Listen. No time for explanations. I want you to do something for me."

"Right," said Pip's voice, sounding excited. "I say – is this a mystery starting up?"

"No. Nothing like that. Listen now. I want you to come up here quickly, unlock my shed, get old Buster out of it, and bring him down to Goon's house. Put him on a lead. Don't come into Goon's – just wait outside till I come out. Tell you everything then!"

Click, Fatty put down the receiver. He rubbed his hands and grinned. Aha, Mr. Goon, you are going to be very, very surprised!

He got into the car beside his father, who glanced at him sideways. "I gather, Frederick," he said, "that you are quite happy about this Buster affair now? But you possibly do not want to tell me why?"

"How right you are, Dad,". said Fatty, cheerfully. "I'll just tell you this: Goon played a very dirty trick, but it's not going to come off!"

There was silence after that. Mr. Trotteville drove straight to Goon's house, and the two of them got out. Goon himself had just arrived, and was astonished to find the house completely empty. No Mrs. Mickle, no Bert!

48

Mr. Trotteville and Fatty went in at the front door, and at the very same moment Mrs. Mickle and Bert arrived at the back. Bert's eyes were red, and he looked frightened. Mrs. Mickle was in a rage.

She spoke to Mr. Goon. "I'm sorry to have left the house so sudden-like, Mr. Goon — but that dratted boy of the butcher's came along and told me I was wanted at home — so I left Bert here in charge, and rushed home — and I wasn't wanted after all. Just wait till I get that butcher's boy!"

Bert gave a sudden sniff. Mrs. Mickle looked at him in disgust. "And Bert — who I left here just to stay till you were back, sir — he come racing home, howling like I don't know what. Scared of being left in your place alone, and telling such tales as I never heard the like of in my life!"

"Mr. Trotteville, this is the boy who caught Buster chasing sheep last night," said Goon.

"I never!" said Bert, suddenly, and burst into tears. "I never, I never!"

"Bert! How can you tell stories like that?" said his mother. "Why, you stood there and told Mr. Goon all about it this morning. I heard you!"

"I never, I never, I never," said Bert, and sniffled again.

"He's a bit nervous, I expect," said Goon, surprised and most displeased. "You caught the dog yourself, didn't you, Bert?"

"I never," said Bert, who seemed quite incapable of saying anything else.

Goon gave it up. "Well, the dog's in the shed, and it's the very dog Bert brought in and put there himself."

"I never!" said Bert, making Mr. Goon long to box his ears. The big policeman strode out through the kitchen and into the garden, taking with him the keys of the shed. He inserted one into the lock, and flung the door open, expecting Buster to rush out and declare himself.

49

But no dog arrived. Instead, Mr. Goon's extremely large black cat strolled out haughtily, sat down outside the shed, and began to wash himself.

Goon's eyes nearly fell out of his head. Fatty gave a roar of laughter and Bert howled in fright. Bert *had* put Buster into the shed; and to see the black cat come out instead of the dog was quite terrifying to poor Bert.

"I never, I never, I never!" he sobbed, and hid his face in his mother's apron.

Goon's mouth opened and shut like a goldfish's, and he couldn't say a word. The cat went on washing itself, and Bert went on howling.

"Well, Mr. Goon, if it's a cat that was shut into this shed, and not Buster, I really don't think it's worthwhile our wasting our time with you any more," said Mr. Trotteville, sounding quite disgusted. "Did you say that you yourself saw the dog that was put into the shed?"

Goon hadn't seen Buster. He had been out when Bert arrived with the dog and he had just taken Bert's word for it. Now he didn't know whether Bert had shut up a dog or the cat. He glared at the boy as if he could bite him.

Bert howled afresh. He put his hand in his pocket and took out half a crown. He held it out to Goon. "Here you are. I've been wicked. Here's the half-crown you gave me, Mr. Goon. I'll never go after dogs again for you."

"Well, I think we've heard enough," said Mr. Trotteville coldly. "Goon, you deserve to be reported for all this. I've a good mind to do so. Come on, Frederick."

"But — but I don't understand it," said Goon, his eyes popping out of his head. "Why, I *heard* that dog barking in the shed, I tell you! Hark! Isn't that him barking now?"

It was! Pip was walking up and down outside, with Buster on the lead, and Buster had recognized Mr. Trotteville's car parked nearby. He was barking his head off in delight.

They all went to the front door – and poor Goon nearly fainted when he saw Buster, Buster himself, pulling on Pip's lead and barking frantically.

"Hallo, Pip," said Fatty, in a very ordinary voice. "Thanks for taking Buster for a walk. Slip him off the lead, will you?"

"No. No, don't," said Goon, finding his voice suddenly. "Wait till I'm indoors."

He shot into the house and slammed the door. Fatty grinned at his father. "I *should* like to know how the cat took the place of the dog," murmured Mr. Trotteville, getting into the car with Fatty and Buster. Pip got in too, puzzled, but grinning all over his face.

"Tell you when we get home," said Fatty. "My word – I wouldn't like to be young Bert right now!"

Young Bert was indeed having a bad time. Mrs. Mickle was crying, Bert was howling, and Goon felt rather like howling himself. He felt a fool, an idiot – to bring that high-and-mighty Mr. Trotteville down to show him a dog locked up in his shed – and then his own black cat walked out! Gah!

Bert told a peculiar tale of voices in every corner, when he had been left alone in the house. Goon looked round uneasily. Voices? What did Bert mean? He suddenly remembered Fatty's ability to throw his voice, just like any ventriloquist. *Could* Fatty have been here? No, impossible!

The more Goon thought about it, the more impossible everything seemed. He looked at Bert with so much dislike that the skinny little boy decided he'd slip off home. What with his Mum cross with him, and Mr. Goon looking as if he'd like to eat him up, and those voices he had heard, life wasn't worth living! So Bert slipped off home.

"I think Pip and I will get out of the car, and have an ice-cream, Dad," said Fatty to his father, as they drove down the main street. "I somehow feel like one. You can have one too, Buster."

"Right," said his father and stopped. "I'm glad Buster's all right, Frederick. I'll hear all about it later."

Fatty and Pip got out with Buster. "I say – do tell me what's been happening! " said Pip.

"Come in here and I'll tell you," said Fatty. "Goon tried to play a very dirty trick – and it didn't come off. Come along."

And over three ice-creams Fatty told the horrified Pip the dreadful story of how Buster had nearly been shot for doing something he hadn't done! Pip almost choked over his ice-cream!

"Look – there's Larry and Daisy and Bets," said Pip, suddenly. "Let's have them in and tell them too."

But it turned out that the other three had already had ice-creams, and were now on their way to fetch something. "Larry left the leather behind in the garden of that bungalow whose windows he cleaned the other day," explained Daisy. "And Mother's been hunting for it everywhere. So we thought we'd better go and find it in the bushes. It's sure to be there still."

"We'll all come – and then you can come back home with me and I'll tell you a most peculiar tale," said Fatty. "*Most* peculiar – isn't it, Buster?"

"Not a mystery, is it?" asked Bets, hopefully, as they all went along together. Fatty shook his head.

"There's not even the smell of a one," he said. "Look – isn't this the place, Larry – that little bungalow there?"

"Yes," said Larry, and went into the garden. He came back quite quickly, looking rather scared.

"I say – there's somebody shouting like anything in that bungalow. It sounds as if they're yelling 'Police! Police! Police!'"

"*Really?* Come on, we'll see what's up," said Fatty, and

they all trooped in at the gate. Fatty went to the door. It was shut. From within came a curious croaking shout.

"Police! Police! Fetch the police!"

"Whatever can be the matter?" said Fatty. "I'd better go in and see!"

The Old Man in the Bungalow

The five children and Buster went up the path. The front door was shut. Fatty went to look in at one of the windows, and the others followed.

Green curtains were drawn back to let the light into the room. In the middle of the room sat an old man in a small arm-chair. He was beating on the arms and shouting "Police! Police! Fetch the police!"

"It's the old man I saw when I cleaned the windows," said Larry. "What's the matter with him? Why does he want the police?"

They all looked at the old fellow. He had on a dressing-gown over pyjamas, and a night-cap that had slipped to one side of his bald head. He had a small beard on his chin and a scarf tied loosely round his neck.

By the stove stood a wheel-chair with a rug half-falling off it, and on a shelf nearby was a small portable radio, within reach of the old man's hand. The children could hear it playing loudly.

"Something's upset the old fellow," said Fatty. "Let's try the door and see if it's unlocked."

They went back to the door, and Fatty turned the handle. The door opened at once.

They all went in, Buster too. The old man neither heard nor saw them. He still sat in the chair, beating its arms, and wailing for the police.

Fatty touched him on the arm, and the old fellow jumped. He stopped shouting and blinked up at Fatty with watery eyes. He put out his hand and felt along Fatty's coat.

"Who is it? Is it the police? Who are you?"

"I'm someone who heard you shouting and came to see what was the matter," said Fatty speaking loudly. "Can we help you? What has happened?"

It was clear that the old man could hardly see. He peered round at the others and drew his dressing-gown around him. He began to shiver.

"Look — you get back to the fire," said Fatty. "I'll take one arm — Larry, you take the other. The old fellow has had a shock of some kind — he's trembling. Turn off that radio, Bets!"

The old man made no objection to being helped to his own chair. He sat down in it with a sigh, and let Daisy arrange his cushions and rug. He peered at them again.

"Who are you all? Fetch the police, I say," he said, and his voice quavered as he spoke.

"Do tell us what's the matter," said Daisy. But he couldn't hear her, and she repeated the question loudly.

"Matter? Matter enough. My money's gone!" he said, and his voice rose to a howl. "All my money! Now what's to happen to me?"

"How do you know it's gone?" said Fatty, loudly. "Didn't you keep it in the bank, or the post-office?"

"Banks! I don't trust banks!" wailed the old fellow. "I hid it where nobody could find it. Now it's gone."

"Where did you hide it?" asked Larry.

"What? What's that?" said the old man, cupping his hand over his ear. "Speak up."

"I said, 'WHERE DID YOU HIDE IT?'" repeated Larry. A sly look came over the old fellow's face. He shook his head.

54

"I shan't tell you. No, that's my secret. It was hidden where nobody could find it. But now it's gone."

"Tell us where you hid it, and we'll have a good look for ourselves," said Daisy loudly. But the old man shook his head more vigorously than ever.

"You get the police!" he said. "I want the police! Two hundred pounds, that's what's gone – all my savings. The police will get it back for me. You get the police."

Fatty didn't in the least want to go and find Mr. Goon. Goon would turn them all out and not let them help at all. He would be bossy and domineering and a perfect nuisance.

"When did you miss the money?" he asked the old man.

"Just now," he said. "About ten minutes ago. I looked for it – and it was gone! Oh, I'm a poor old man and people have robbed me! Get the police."

"We will," said Fatty, comfortingly. "Just tell us when you *last* saw the money. Do you remember?"

"Course I remember," said the old fellow, pulling his night-cap straight. "But I didn't *see* it. I'm nearly blind. I *felt* it. It was there all right."

"When was that?" asked Fatty, patiently.

"Last night," said the old man. "About midnight, I reckon. I was in bed, and I couldn't sleep, and I sat up and worried about my money. You see, I'm all alone here since my daughter's gone away. Well, I got out of bed and I came in here. And I felt for my money. It was there all right."

"I see," said Fatty. "So somebody must have taken it between then and now. Has anyone been to see you this morning?"

"Yes. Yes, of course," he said. "But I'm muddled now. I misremember who came – except my granddaughter, of course – she comes every day and cleans round. She's a good girl. And the grocer came. But I misremember. You

55

get the police. They'll find my money for me!'"

A big tear fell from one eye and rolled down his cheek. Bets felt very sorry for him. Poor old man – all alone, and worried about his money. Where could it be? Had it really been stolen – or had he just forgotten where he had put it? If only he would tell them!

"We'll have to tell Goon," said Fatty to the others. "It's a pity. We might have been able to clear this up ourselves if we'd had a chance."

The five children suddenly heard footsteps coming up the path. Who was it? There was a loud knock at the door, then the handle turned, and a man walked in. He stared in surprise at the children. Buster barked loudly.

"Hallo!" said the man. He was young and smartly dressed. "Who are you? Are you visiting my great-uncle! Hallo, Uncle! How are you?"

"Oh, Wilfrid – is it you?" said the old man, putting out a hand as if to find out where Wilfrid was. "Wilfrid, my money's gone!"

"What! Gone? What do you mean?" asked Wilfrid. "Didn't I tell you somebody would rob you if you didn't let me put it into the bank for you?"

"It's gone, it's gone," said his uncle, rocking himself to and fro.

"Where did you keep it?" asked Wilfrid, looking all round. "I bet it's not gone, Uncle! You've forgotten where you hid it! Maybe up the chimney – or under a floor-board?"

"I'm not telling anyone," said the old man. "I want the police! I'm tired. I want my money and I want the police!'"

"We'll go and telephone for the police, if you like," Fatty offered. "I see there are telephone wires leading next door. I expect they'd let me use the phone."

"What are *you* doing here, anyway?" said Wilfrid, suddenly.

56

"Nothing. We just heard the old man calling," said Fatty, thinking it better not to say that Larry had gone to find the leather he had left behind in the bushes, and had heard the old man shouting as he passed the bungalow. "Anyway, we'll go and telephone now. The police will be up in a few minutes, I'm sure."

"Good-bye," said Bets to the old man, but he didn't hear her. He was moaning softly to himself. "My money! Now what shall I do? All gone, all gone!"

The five of them went out with Buster. They went down the path and walked beside the fence till they came to Green-Trees. They went up the path to the blue front door. Fatty rang the bell.

A pleasant-faced woman answered it. She looked very French, and Fatty decided that she must be the sister whose house the bundled-up man had tried so hard to find.

"Excuse me," said Fatty, politely. "Do you think I might use your telephone? The old man in the bungalow next door has been robbed, and we want to tell the police."

The woman looked startled. "A robbery? Next door? Oh, the poor old man! Yes, come in and use my telephone! It is in this room here."

She spoke English extremely well, but had a slight accent which was rather pleasant. She was very like her brother, dark and plump.

She took them into a room off the hall. A couch stood by the window, and a man lay on it coughing. He turned as they came in.

"Henri, these children want to use the telephone," said the woman. "You do not mind?"

"Enter, I pray you," said the man, and then stared. "Ah!" he said, "zeese children I have seen before – n'est-ce-pas?"

"Yes," said Fatty. "We guided you to Green-Trees, you remember?"

"Yes — Grintriss," said the man with a smile. He looked quite different now, without his bulky overcoat, scarf and pulled-down hat — younger and pleasanter. He coughed. "You will pardon me if I lie here? I am not so well."

"Of course," said Fatty. "I hope you don't mind our coming here like this — but the old fellow next door has been robbed of his money — or so he says — and we want to tell the police."

Fatty took up the receiver of the telephone. "Police Station," he said.

A loud, sharp voice answered. "P.C. Goon here. Who's calling?"

"Er — Frederick Trotteville," said Fatty. "I just wanted to tell you that..."

There was a loud snort from the other end and a crash. Goon had put down his receiver in a temper! Fatty was astonished.

"Gosh! I got Goon, and as soon as I began to speak to him he crashed back the receiver!" said Fatty. "I suppose he's still furious about Buster. Well, I'll try again."

He got the police station once more, and again Goon's voice answered.

"Look here, Mr. Goon," said Fatty. "Will you go to the bungalow called Hollies, in Holly Lane. There's been a robbery there."

"Any more of your nonsense and I'll report you to Headquarters," snapped Goon. "I'm not going out on any wild-goose-chase, and have you come back here and shut my cat up in the shed again. Ho, yes, I..."

"MR. GOON! LISTEN!" shouted Fatty. "This isn't a joke, it's..."

Crash! Goon had put down his receiver again. Fatty put down his and stared in comical dismay at the others. "Goon's mad! He thinks I'm spoofing him. What shall we do?"

"Ring up Superintendent Jenks," suggested Daisy. "It's the only thing to do, Fatty!"

"I will!" said Fatty. "It'll serve Goon right!"

Goon takes Charge

Fatty rang through to Police Headquarters in the next town, and asked for Superintendent Jenks.

"He's out," said a voice. "Who wants him?"

"Er – this is Frederick Trotteville," said Fatty, wishing the Superintendent was in. "I just wanted to say that a robbery has been committed at a bungalow called Hollies, in Holly Lane, Peterswood, and the old man who's been robbed asked me to tell the police."

"You want to ring up *Peterswood* Police then," said the voice.

"I have," said Fatty. "I – er – I can't seem to get hold of them. Perhaps you could ring through to tell them?"

"Right," said the voice. "Robbery – Hollies – Holly Lane – Peterswood. And your name is –?"

"Frederick Trotteville," said Fatty.

"Ah, yes – I know! Friend of the Super, aren't you?" said the voice, in a more friendly tone. "Right, sir – leave it to me."

And so once more the telephone rang at Goon's house, and once more he answered it, snatching it up angrily, sure that it was Fatty again.

"Hallo, hallo! Who's that?" he barked.

A surprised voice answered. "This is Headquarters. Is that P.C. Goon? A boy called Frederick Trotteville has just . . ."

"Pah!" said Goon, unable to help himself.

"What did you say?" said the voice, still more surprised.

"Nothing. Just coughed," said Goon. "What about this here boy?"

"He reports a robberty at the bungalow called Hollies, Holly Lane, in your area," said the voice.

Goon's mouth fell open. So Fatty hadn't been trying to spoof him! There really had been a robbery. What a pest of a boy! Playing tricks on him and Bert — and the cat — and getting away with Buster — and now finding a robbery! What a Toad of a boy!

"Are you there?" said the voice, impatiently. "Have you got what I said?"

"Er — yes — yes," said Goon, scribbling down a few notes. "Thanks. All right. I'll go right along."

"You'd better!" said the voice, puzzled and annoyed. There was a click. Goon stared at the telephone and clicked back his receiver too. Now he'd get a rap on the knuckles for making Fatty ring Headquarters. Why hadn't he listened to him when he telephoned?

He got out his bicycle and yelled to Mrs. Mickle. "Be back in half an hour, I expect. Have my dinner ready! This is an urgent job."

The five children had not left Green-Trees by the time Goon cycled up. They were talking to the Frenchman, whose name turned out to be Henri Crozier. They told him all about the old fellow next door.

"I can see the front gate and front path of the bungalow from my couch," said Henri. "I got my sister to put the couch here because it's a pleasant view, and I can see people who come and go down the road."

They all looked out of the window. "You must have seen us going in, then," said Fatty. "Did you?"

"Oh, yes," said Henri. "First I saw zis boy — what does he call himself — Larry? He went in and up the path — and then he came running back to you, and you all went up the path and in at the front-door."

Larry went red. He hoped to goodness that Henri wasn't going to ask him why he had first gone in at the gate. It wouldn't be at all easy to explain how it was that he had left a window-leather in the bushes!

Fortunately his sister came bustling in just then. Her name was Mrs. Harris and her husband, who was away, was English. She carried a box of French chocolates, very rich and creamy.

"Oh – thanks," said Daisy, and took one. They all helped themselves, and then there came a sudden exclamation from Henri.

"See – the police have arrived!"

Sure enough, Mr. Goon was wheeling his bicycle up the front path next door. The door opened as he came and the young man, Wilfrid, appeared. He said something to Goon and they both disappeared into the bungalow.

"Well, now, perhaps the old man will be happy," said Fatty. "My word – what super chocolate! We don't get chocolates like that here, Mrs. Harris."

"We'd better go," said Pip, looking at his watch. "Do you know it's almost one o'clock? Good gracious! Mother said we must be back by five to. Buck up, Bets."

The five said good-bye to Henri and his sister. "You will come again?" said the sister. "Henri is so bored. He has been very ill and now he comes to me to – how do you call it? – to convalesce. Come and see him again."

"Thank you. We will," said Fatty, hoping fervently that Mr. Goon would not also take it into his head to go and see Henri and his sister, and ask them if they had noticed visitors at the bungalow that morning! It might be very awkward to explain Larry's visit there an hour or so before. Blow that window-leather! And yet, if Larry hadn't gone to find it, he wouldn't have heard the old man shouting.

"Gosh – I never got Mother's window-leather after all!"

61

said Larry. "What an idiot I am. I'll slip in and get it now."

"No, you won't," said Fatty, firmly. "You'll leave it there. We don't want Goon to come rushing out and asking you what you're doing. You can get it when Goon's not there."

They all went home. Fatty was thinking hard. Why wouldn't the old man say where he had hidden his money? It was silly of him, because he might have made a mistake when he hunted for it – it might quite well still be in the bungalow in some place he had forgotten.

"Larry said that the old fellow was crawling about, feeling under the furniture, the day he went to clean the windows," thought Fatty. "Why feel so *much* of the furniture? Did he sometimes put the money in one place and sometimes in another? Or perhaps he divided it up – it might be in notes – and put in several places. That's quite likely. Well, it's not a *real* mystery – only an ordinary robbery. Goon will soon find the robber. He's only got to get a list of the people who visited the bungalow this morning, and weed them out."

That afternoon Goon arrived at Fatty's house. He asked for Fatty – and Jane showed him into the study.

"That fat policeman wants you, Master Frederick," said Jane, when she found Fatty. "I hope Buster hasn't got into trouble again!"

"Wuff," said Buster, and danced round Jane. Fatty debated whether to take the little Scottie into the study with him or not. He thought he would. It might keep Goon in his place!

So in marched Fatty, with Buster at his heels. Goon was standing at the window, frowning. He was feeling angry about a lot of things. He was angrier still when he felt Buster sniffing at his heels.

"Come here, Buster," said Fatty. "Oh, won't you sit down, Mr. Goon? Anything I can do for you?"

Goon swung round, eyeing Buster balefully. That dog! Had that tiresome Bert locked him up the shed the night before, or hadn't he? He couldn't get a word out of Bert now.

Goon sat down heavily and took out his bulky notebook. "I've come about the robbery," he said.

"Well, I'm not guilty," said Fatty, smoothly. "I do assure you I..."

"I know you're not guilty," said Goon, looking as if he wished Fatty were. "What I want to know is – how did you come to be around there just when the old man was yelling blue murder?"

"He wasn't," corrected Fatty. "He was yelling for the police."

"Pah!" said Goon. "You know what I mean. Seems a funny thing to me the way you kids are always about when anything happens. Snooping round. Prying. Interfering with the Law."

"If that's all you've come to tell me you might as well say good-bye," said Fatty, getting up. "I mean, I can easily bike over to the Superintendent this afternoon and tell *him* everything. I don't want to interfere with the Law. I want to help it. We couldn't help being there just at that moment. Well, good morning, Mr. Goon."

Goon looked extremely startled. "Now, you sit down," he said, trying to speak pleasantly. "I'm only just saying what a remarkable thing it is that you always seem to be around when these things happen. Nothing wrong in saying that, is there?"

"You mentioned something about snooping. And prying," said Fatty.

"Ah, well, I'm a bit upset-like," said Mr. Goon, taking out an enormous handkerchief and wiping his forehead with it. "Let's forget it. I don't want to interview you, but the law's the law. It's the last thing I want to do today –

63

see you again. But I've got to ask you a few questions seeing as you and the others were the first on the spot, so to speak."

"Ask away," said Fatty, "but don't be too verbose – I've got plenty to do."

Goon wondered what "verbose" meant – something rude, he'd be bound! He determined to look it up in the dictionary when he got back. Verbose!

He began to ask Fatty a few routine questions.

"What time had Fatty and the others been there? Anyone about? Anything disarranged in the living-room? What had the old man said?"

Fatty answered shortly and truthfully, thankful that Goon had no suspicion that they had actually gone to the bungalow garden to fetch something. Goon imagined that they had been out for a walk, and had heard the old man's yells as they passed.

"That's all," said Goon, at last. Fatty thought that he had asked the questions very well. He had left nothing out that might be useful.

Goon loked at Fatty. "Er – I suppose you've got your own ideas about this already?" he said.

"Oh, yes," said Fatty. "I've no doubt it will be quite easy to find the robber. Didn't the old man give you a list of the people who had been to visit him this morning?"

"Well, he seemed so muddled," said Goon. "He might have been remembering *yesterday's* visitors. He's old and forgetful. I wouldn't be surprised if that money isn't still there somewhere. Er – hm – what do you think about it all?"

Fatty wasn't going to give Goon any help at all. He remembered how Goon had given Bert half a crown to catch Buster. He got up suddenly, not wanting to look at the fat policeman any more.

"Good morning," he said to Goon, and showed him out

very firmly. Let Goon find out what he could — Fatty didn't mean to help him!·

Tea at Pip's

The Five met that day in Pip's playroom at half-past three. Mrs. Hilton had said they might all go to tea, and had sent Pip and Bets out to buy cakes from the baker's.

They had staggered in with baskets full, and had arranged all the goodies themselves on big dishes. They were set on the table, ready for tea.

"Why do you put them under our noses like this?" groaned Daisy. "*Look* at those macaroons — all goey and luscious. What a frightful temptation."

"And look at that gingerbread cake — and that fruit cake," said Larry. "We never seem to have such nice teas as you do, Pip."

"Oh, it's only when people come to tea that Mother goes a splash like this," said Pip. "Buster, you've got your favourite tit-bit — dog-biscuits spread with potted meat. Sniff!"

Buster sniffed, shot out a pink tongue — and the biscuit disappeared with one crunch!

"Oh, Buster! Manners, manners!" said Fatty. "You don't see your master doing things like that, do you?"

·Everyone laughed. Pip got out some cards and shuffled them. Fatty told them of Goon's visit to him that afternoon.

"How you could bear to be polite to him when you knew he had planned to have Buster shot, I *don't* know!" said Pip.

"Well, I *wasn't* awfully polite, actually," admitted Fatty. "Also I was a bit afraid he'd ask why we were there. I

65

wish to goodness you'd taken away that window-leather, Larry. I wouldn't put it past old Goon to snoop round the garden and find it."

"Blow!" said Larry. "Mother keeps on asking about it. I really must get it soon. I would have bought a new one, but when Daisy and I looked in the ironmonger's shop this afternoon, the big ones were about fifteen shillings. Fifteen shillings! I call that wicked."

"I'll get it from the bungalow garden for you," said Fatty. "You mustn't go bursting in at the garden gate in full daylight, and come out waving a window-leather! I'll go tonight and get it, when it's dark."

"I shouldn't have gone in daylight anyhow," said Larry, a little offended. "I'm not *quite* an idiot. But I'd be glad if you got it for me, actually, because it's difficult for me to slip out at night. It's easy for you – you can always say you're taking Buster for a walk."

"I ususally do take him for a run last thing at night," said Fatty. "I'll go tonight, and I'll bring the leather here to you tomorrow."

"Are we going to go and see that old man again?" asked Daisy. "Are we going to treat this as a mystery – a rather small one, I know – and try to find out who the robber is, or are we going to let Goon get on with it, and not bother about it at all ourselves?"

"Well, I don't actually think there's much mystery," said Fatty. "Either the money is still there, hidden, and the old fellow has forgotten where, or someone's taken it who knew it was hidden. If so, it can only be one of his relatives, I should think. Quite a straightforward case. Anyway I somehow don't want to have anything more to do with Goon, after this Buster business. I just can't bear the sight of him."

"Right. Then we don't count this as a mystery," said Daisy. "We'll just go on hoping. What I *was* going to say was that the person who would really know who visited the old man this morning would be that Frenchman – Mr. Henri. He lies on that couch and watches everyone who passes – and he has a jolly good view of the bungalow's front door."

"Yes. You're right," said Fatty. "He would be the first one we'd ask for a bit of information. But I think we'll leave this to Goon. To tell you the truth, I'm a bit afraid of somebody asking about a window-cleaner! Somebody may have spotted Larry – and we'd look rather foolish if it came out about his cleaning the windows."

"I always thought it was rather a silly thing to ask me to do," said Larry. "I said so at the time."

"Well, maybe it was a bit mad," said Fatty. "We'll forget it. Come on – whose deal is it? We'll just have time for a game before tea."

They had a hilarious game, and an even more hilarious tea. During the game, Buster discovered that by sitting on a chair, he could reach his plate of potted-meat biscuits, and he devoured every one of them without being noticed. He then quietly jumped down and went and lay by Bets.

"Isn't he good and quiet today?" said Bets, patting him. "He's usually too silly for words when we play cards and don't take any notice of him. Last time he smacked all my cards out of my hand, I remember. Didn't you, Buster?"

"Wuff," said Buster, in a quiet voice. He was beginning to feel very guilty.

Larry tickled him. Buster didn't jump up and caper round as he usually did. He just let Larry tickle him. Larry looked at him closely.

"Why don't you wag your tail?" he said. "I say – don't you think Buster's gone rather quiet? Buster, old fellow, what's up?"

Buster's tail remained quite still, without a wag. Bets looked at him in alarm. "He can't be feeling well! Buster!

Good dog! Stand up, Buster, and wag your tail!"

Buster stood up, looking the picture of misery, head down and tail down. What a fuss the children made of him! He was patted and petted, stroked and fondled.

"Ought we to take him to the vet?" said Bets. "Fatty, do you think anything's wrong?"

"We'll try him with one of his favourite potted-meat biscuits," said Fatty, getting up. He saw the empty plate at once.

"BUSTER! You greedy pig! How dare you show such bad manners when I take you out to tea! I'm ashamed of you. Go to the corner!"

"Oh, what's he done?" cried Bets, as poor Buster walked to the nearest corner, and sat there, face to the wall.

"Eaten every single one of his biscuits whilst we weren't looking," said Fatty. "I never heard a single crunch, did you? Bad dog, Buster! No, Bets, you're not to go to him. Look at the plate next to his biscuits, too. It looks as if Buster has been taking a few licks at that macaroon!"

"Well, I'd rather he was naughty than ill," said Bets, making up her mind to slip Buster a bit of macaroon at tea-time. "Oh, Buster! What a thing to do!"

Buster made a moaning sound, and hung his head still more. "Take no notice of him," said Fatty, "another word from us and he'll burst into tears."

"It wouldn't matter. He'd lick them all up," said Bets. "That's the best of being a dog – if you upset a dish you can always lick up the mess."

"Now don't even mention Buster's name," said Fatty, firmly. "He's in disgrace. Come on – it's my turn to play."

Buster had to remain in the corner while the five children had their own tea. Bets spilt some runny strawberry jam on the clean tablecloth.

"Get something to wipe it," said Pip. "You really are a messer, Bets."

"I'm a dog. I'm going to lick it up," said Bets, and she did, which made them all laugh. Tea became more and more hilarious until Pip laughed so much that he fell off his chair and pulled a plate of cake-slices on top of him.

The door opened and Mrs. Hilton looked in. "What was that crash?" she said. "Is anybody hurt? Oh, *Pip!* What *are* you doing on the floor with cakes all over you? Please get up. Remember you are the host."

"Be hostly, Pip," said Bets, and Pip began to laugh again. Buster came out of his corner hopefully when he saw the pieces of cake on the floor.

"No, Buster, the floor is perfectly clean and we can eat the slices ourselves, thank you," said Pip. "Has Mother gone? Oh, dear, I really must be hostly. Shall we let Buster stay out of his corner? I'm sure he must be very sorry now."

So, much to Buster's joy, he was allowed to join the others again, and was so pleased to be in favour that he went round licking everyone in all the bare places he could find.

"Really, we need a towel!" said Daisy. "That's the third time you've licked my knees, Buster — they're dripping with lick!"

The evening went too quickly. Fatty exclaimed when he looked at the playroom clock. "Whew! Almost seven o'clock. You have your supper at seven, don't you, Pip?"

"Gosh, yes. And we've got to go and wash and get tidy," said Pip, scrambling up. "Sorry to rush you off; but you know what our household's like — everything on the dot. The gong will go in a minute. See yourselves out, will you!"

Fatty, Larry, Daisy and Buster went downstairs quietly and out of the garden door. It was getting dark. "It's a pity we haven't a mystery on hand," said Larry, lighting his bicycle lamp. "I feel like one, somehow. It's nice when we've got our teeth into a good, juicy mystery!"

"Well, one may turn up at any time," said Fatty. "Your lamp all right, Daisy? Good-bye, then. We'll see each other sometime tomorrow."

They all cycled off, parting at the corner. Fatty yawned. He had slept very little the night before because he had been so worried about Buster. He felt very sleepy now.

"I'll go to bed early," he thought. "I'll take a book and read. I'll soon be asleep."

So, much to his parent's surprise — for Fatty was usually rather a late bird — he went up to bed about a quarter to nine, with Buster at his heels.

He had a bath, and was soon settled into bed. He opened his book and read a page or two — and then, before he had even turned out his light, he was fast asleep! Half-past nine struck. Ten o'clock. Half-past ten. Eleven. Everyone in the house was now in bed, and Fatty's light was the only one left on.

Buster lay quiet for some time. Then he stirred. Why hadn't Fatty taken him out for a run? He leapt on the bed and woke Fatty up with a jump.

"Gosh, it's you, you little wretch!" said Fatty, sitting up suddenly. "I thought you were a burglar or something. What's the time — almost half-past eleven! Now don't say you want a walk at this hour, because you won't get one. I'm going to turn out the light, see?"

It was just as he switched off his lamp that Fatty remembered something. "Blow, blow, blow! I never went to get that horrible window-leather. BLOW!"

He thought about it. Well, he *must* go and get it. He had promised Larry — and, anyway, it was important. He swung his feet out of bed and dressed hurriedly. "We'll be back soon," he said to Buster. "We'll only be a few minutes!"

But he wasn't back soon. Fatty had a most peculiar midnight adventure!

Fatty went cautiously down the stairs with Buster. Buster always knew when he had to be quiet. He almost held his breath as he padded downstairs at Fatty's heels!

"Out of the garden door, Buster," whispered Fatty, and Buster led the way down the side-passage. Fatty unlocked and unbolted the door quietly, and closed it again. He locked it behind him.

Then he and Buster made their way to the back-gate and slipped out into the road.

Buster liked this. It was exciting to be all alone with Fatty late at night. Smells seemed much stronger than in the day-time. Shadows were more exciting. Buster jumped up and gave Fatty's hand a small lick.

"We're going to that bungalow called Hollies," Fatty told him. "Got to collect something for Larry. If I can't find it, *you'll* have to sniff about for it, Buster."

"Wuff," said Buster, happily, and ran on ahead. Up this way – down that – round a corner – and by a lamp-post. The street-lights went off at twelve. Soon it would be midnight, and then there would not be even a lamp to break the darkness.

It was a very cloudy night, and the clouds were low and thick. Fatty felt a spot of rain. He put his hand in his pocket to make sure he had his torch. Between the lamp-posts the way was very dark. Yes, his torch was there – good.

"I'll need it when I creep into the bungalow garden," thought Fatty. "I'll never find Larry's leather without a light."

He came to the turning into Holly Lane. The street lamps

71

suddenly went out — twelve o'clock! Fatty got out his torch. He simply couldn't see a step in front of him without it on this dark night.

He came to the front gate of the little bungalow. It was all in darkness. Fatty stood and listened. Not a sound could be heard. He could go and search in safety.

He opened the front gate, shut it softly, and went up the path with Buster. He turned off to the side of the bungalow and went into the little thicket of bushes there. He switched on his torch and began to hunt around.

He couldn't see the window-leather anywhere. Blow Larry! He came up against a fence — the fence that separated the bungalow garden from the one belonging to Mr. Henri's sister. He stood and considered the matter.

"Could the wind possibly have blown the leather over the fence?" he wondered. "No. Leathers are such heavy things when wet, as Larry's was. On the other hand, the wind might have dried it, and it would then become dry and light. The wind *might* take it then — there has been quite a breeze."

Fatty climbed over the fence, torch in hand. He hunted all about the garden there. It was very much tidier than the garden of Hollies. He began to get into a panic. Where was this tiresome leather? Surely Goon hadn't found it?

He heard a noise and switched off his torch. It was the sound of a car-engine coming up the road. Fatty thought he would wait for the car to pass, and then have one more look.

But the car didn't pass. It seemed to stop quite nearby. Fatty frowned. Why didn't the car go through some gateway, and on into its own garage, so late at night?

Then he remembered that there was a doctor's house opposite. Possibly the doctor had come home for something, and gone into his house for it. He would come back in a few minutes and drive off again to a patient.

72

So Fatty crouched under a bush and waited, with Buster by his side. The car's engine had been turned off. Fatty could hear no footsteps at all. But he suddenly thought he could hear a bump or two – and surely that was somebody panting?

He was puzzled. It all sounded rather nearer than the doctor's house. Surely the car wasn't outside *Hollies*? If so – what was going on?

Fatty crept back to the fence that separated the two gardens. He climbed over it cautiously, lifting Buster up too, and putting him down in the bungalow garden.

"Ssh, Buster!" he whispered. "Quiet now!"

Buster froze still. He gave a tiny growl as if to say "Funny goings-on somewhere!" then was quite quiet. Fatty crept between the bushes, and stopped suddenly.

He could see a torch bobbing along about two feet above the front path. Somebody was there, carrying it – somebody who was panting hard. Somebody who wore rubber-soled shoes, too, for not a footstep could be heard!

Fatty suddenly heard a whisper. So there were *two* people then? Who were they? And what in the world were they doing? Surely they weren't kidnapping the old man?

Fatty frowned. He had better find out about that poor fellow. He slept in the back room of the bungalow. That was where Larry had seen his bed.

"If I slip round to the back, and shine my torch in at the window, I could perhaps see if the old man is there or not," he thought. So he crept round the bushes once more and came to the back of the little bungalow.

The window was open. Fatty was just about to shine his torch through the opening when he heard a noise.

Someone was snoring! Snoring very loudly indeed! The old man was safe then. Fatty stood and listened for a while, and then made his way back into the bushes. He really *must* see what was up!

He heard the sound of the front door closing very quietly. He heard a tiny little cough, but he caught no sound of footsteps going down to the gate. He stood and listened, his ears straining for the slightest noise.

He heard another door being shut – the door of the car, perhaps. Yes, that was it. Then the car-engine started up suddenly, and began to throb. Almost at once the car moved off down the road. Fatty leapt to the front fence and shone his torch on it. He saw only a dark shadow as the car drove away. His torch could not even pick out the number.

"What a peculiar business," thought Fatty. "What did those fellows come to fetch – or perhaps they *brought* something? I'll go and peep in at the front windows."

But thick curtains of some green material stretched across the front windows, with not a crack between them to shine his light through. Fatty went to the front door and tried it.

No, that was now locked. It was all most mysterious. What were the midnight visitors doing in the bungalow?

Fatty went to the back and took another look through the window. This time he shone his torch on the old man. Yes, there he was on his bed, fast asleep, his night-cap all crooked. Beside him was a plain chair, and a small table. There didn't seem to be anything else in the room at all.

Fatty switched off his torch, and went round to the front. He was puzzled to know what to do for the best. He didn't like to wake the old man; he would be sure to be in a terrible fright if Fatty awoke him suddenly – and how was Fatty to explain to him about the midnight visitors? The old man would be so terrified that he wouldn't go to sleep again!

"It will have to wait till morning," said Fatty to himself. "I'm not going to ring up Goon. For one thing he wouldn't believe me – for another thing there may be a simple explanation – and for a third thing I can't see that it will matter waiting till morning."

So he went off with Buster at his heels, puzzled, and half-doubtful about leaving the old man all by himself, with midnight visitors coming and going!

He let himself in at the garden-door, and he and Buster went upstairs very quietly. They disturbed nobody. Buster curled up at once in his basket and went to sleep.

Fatty lay awake thinking over everything for a few minutes, and then fell off to sleep as suddenly as Buster. He didn't wake till full daylight. The breakfast gong was sounding through the house. Fatty leapt out of bed in a hurry!

"Gosh, I must have been sleepy!" he said. He stirred Buster with a bare foot. "Wake up, sleepy head! You're as bad as I am!"

He didn't remember about his midnight adventure for a minute or two, he was so much engrossed in dressing as quickly as he could. Then he suddenly remembered and stopped tying his tie. "Whew! Was it a dream, or real? Buster, do you remember our midnight walk, too? If you do, it was real."

Buster did remember. He gave a small wuff, and leapt on Fatty's warm bed.

"Get down," said Fatty. "Well, I'm glad you remember our walk last night, too. Funny business, wasn't it, Buster? Shall we pop round to that bungalow immediately after breakfast, just to see what's happened – if anything?"

So, after breakfast, Fatty got his bicycle and set off slowly with Buster running beside him, panting. "This will do you good, Tubby-One," said Fatty, severely. "Why is it that you always get so fat when I'm away at school? Can't you possibly go for walks by yourself?"

Buster was too much out of breath even to bark. Fatty

turned into Holly Lane, and rode up to the bungalow. The door was shut, but the green curtains were now pulled back from the windows. Fatty peeped in to see if things were all right.

He got a terrible shock! Mr. Goon was there – a most important Mr. Goon – and with him was Mr. Henri from next door! The old man was nowhere to be seen.

But what startled Fatty most was that there was not a stick of furniture in the front room! It was completely empty – not even a carpet on the floor!

He stood gaping in at the window Mr. Goon swung round and saw him. He stepped to the window and flung it open, scowling.

"You here again! What have you come for? Nobody knows about this yet!"

"What's happened?" said Fatty.

Mr. Henri began to explain. "About seven o'clock zis morning," he said, but Mr. Goon interrupted him. He didn't want Fatty to know more than could be helped. Interfering Toad!

Fatty wasn't going to be put off, however. He had to know about this. He spoke rapidly to Mr. Henri in French, asking him to reply in French and tell him everything.

So, to the accompaniment of Mr. Goon's scowls and snorts, Mr. Henri explained everything in French. He had awakened at seven o'clock that morning and had heard somebody yelling. His bedroom faced towards the bungalow. At first he hadn't taken much notice and fell asleep again.

"Then," he said, in his rapid French, "then I awoke later and the noise was still there – shouting, shouting, always. So I dressed and came to the bungalow to see what was the matter."

"Go on," said Fatty.

"It was the old man shouting," said Mr. Henri, still in

French. "The door was locked so I got him to unlock it – and when I came inside, I saw that this room was quite empty – except for the curtains, which had been drawn across the windows so that nobody might see into the empty room. The old had awakened this morning, and staggered out to this room – and when he found everything gone, he yelled the place down!"

"It's a mystery!" said Fatty, amazed, and Goon swung round sharply. "Mr. Goon – we're in the middle of a mystery again! Got any clues?"

Suspects—and Clues!

Mr. Goon didn't feel that he could possibly stand any cheek from Fatty at that moment. He was completely mystified, he had no clues at all, and he simply couldn't *imagine* when, how or why all the front-room furniture had been removed.

"You clear orf," he said to Fatty. "This has got nothing to do with you. It's a job for the police."

"I must just go and see how the poor old man is," said Fatty, and brushed past Goon to go to the back bedroom. Goon scowled. He looked round the room helplessly. Except for the stove, which kept alight all night, the fender one lamp, and the green curtains, there was nothing left in the room. What was the point of taking all the furniture away? It wasn't worth much anyway!

Fatty was talking to the old man, who was almost weeping with shock. "My money first – then my furniture!" he moaned. "All my money – then my furniture! What's to become of me?"

"Didn't you hear anybody?" asked Fatty.

"No, no! Not a thing did I hear," he said. Fatty stopped

questioning him. It was plain that he was too upset to say anything sensible.

Mr. Goon made a few notes in his black book. "I must know the granddaughter's address," he said. "She'll 'ave to come along here and take this old fellow to her home. He can't stay here alone, with no furniture. Hey, Dad! What's your granddaughter's address?"

"It be 5, Marlins Grove, Marlow," said the old man. "But you won't get me there, that you won't. It's full of pesky old women, always grumbling and nagging. I'm not going there."

"But you can't stay here all alone with no furniture!" shouted Mr. Goon, half because the old man was deaf, and half because he was angry.

"Don't yell at him like that," said Fatty, seeing the poor old fellow cower back. Mr. Henri touched Goon on the shoulder.

"My sistair, she is vairy kind," he said in his broken English. "She has a small bedroom. Zis old man can stay there till his granddaughter arrives."

"Well, that would help a bit," said Goon, putting his notebook away. "Will you lock up after you? I must go back to my house and telephone all this to my chief. It's a funny business – can't make it out – first the money, then the furniture!"

He turned to Fatty. "And you'd better go home," he said. "There's no call for you to meddle in this. Always snooping round. What made you come up here this morning I just can't think. Wherever I find trouble I find you!"

It took quite a time to explain to the trembling old man that the people next door would help him. But when he understood he seemed to think he would like to go there. Mr. Henri went to tell his "sistair" everything, and sent a gardener to help Fatty to take the old fellow to his house.

Between them they carried him there, and kind Mrs. Harris soon got him into a warm bed.

"I'll just keep him warm here, till his people come," she said. "I don't mind driving him over to Marlow if it will help. What an extraordinary thing to happen – taking away his furniture in the middle of the night. I never heard even the smallest noise!"

Fatty went back to the bungalow. He had a good look round. He was just as puzzled as Mr. Goon. There was no doubt that the old man had hidden his money somewhere in his furniture – perhaps in several places – but the money had gone.

"So WHY take the furniture!" wondered Fatty. "We'll have to get busy on this – there should be at least a few clues – and everyone who visited the old man yesterday morning up to the time he discovered that his money was gone is on the list of suspects."

Fatty examined the bedroom. The bed was a plain iron one with an ordinary wire spring. Nobody could ever hide money in that. The mattress was thin and poor. Money might have been hidden in that – but no, it would have to be sewn up again each time the old man took it out. He was too blind to do that. Anyway it was clear that nobody had unsewn and then re-sewn the mattress. All the threads were dirty, and had obviously been untouched for years.

The pillow was thin and hard. Fatty took it off the slip and looked at it. No – nobody had ripped the pillow and re-sewn it.

He looked at the floor-board. There were no marks anywhere to show that any had been taken up. All were nailed down fast. The chimney-place was no good for hiding anything either. The stove fitted too closely.

"Well, it beats me. WHY did somebody take the risk of coming at midnight and carrying out all the furniture, when the money had obviously been stolen?" said Fatty. "Unless

— unless — they were sure it was still there, somewhere in the furniture! They didn't like to risk coming and making a really good search, so they took *all* the furniture, meaning to search it at leisure."

He thought about that. "No, that seems silly. But then everything seems a bit silly. Buster, don't you think this is rather a *silly* mystery?"

"Wuff, wuff," said Buster, quite agreeing. He wasn't very interested in this little house. Not even the smell of a mouse! He pawed at Fatty's leg.

"All right. I'm coming," said Fatty. "I'll just lock the door. I'd better leave the key with Mr. Henri."

He locked the door, and then went to have one more look for Larry's leather in the daylight. No, it was gone. He hoped that Larry wouldn't get into trouble over it.

Fatty made his way to the house next door, after fixing a bit of paper to the front door of Hollies. On it he had written "KEY NEXT DOOR" just in case the grand-daughter should come back.

Mrs. Harris answered the door and told him to come in. "We are having a cup of coffee," she said. "You must join us. My brother would like a word with you too."

Fatty also wanted a word with Mr. Henri. He thought it would be distinctly useful to have a list of all the people that Mr. Henri had seen going to the Hollies the morning before. One of those people must have been the thief who took the money.

Mr. Henri was ready to tell all he knew. He was just as much interested in the matter as Fatty was. He had already made a neat list, and he showed it to Fatty.

Fatty ran his eyes down it. There were six people on the list.

1 Lady with papers or magazines.
2 Window-Cleaner.

3 *Grocer's Boy.*

4 *Man in car, number ERT 100. Carried bag.*

5 *Man, well-dressed, young, stayed for only a minute.*

6 *Young woman, stayed a long time.*

Fatty read the list again. "Quite a long list," he said. "It will be a bit of a business checking all these. I wonder if the old man could help a bit with some of them."

"He said his granddaughter came to do some cleaning," said Mr. Henri, "so that must be the 'young woman.' And he says he thinks his nephew came – but he's so muddled. He doesn't seem to remember any of the others. I can give you more details, of course. For instance, the woman with the magazines of papers wore a red coat and had a hat with red roses in."

"Yes – all the details would be a help," said Fatty. "What about the grocer's boy?"

"He came on a bicycle with the name of 'WELBURN' on the front of the basket," said Mr. Henri, who seemed a remarkably observant fellow. "A red-haired boy."

"Did you notice if the window-cleaner had a name on his pail or bicycle?" asked Fatty, wondering if the cleaner had noticed how remarkably clean the windows of Hollies had been! After all, Larry had cleaned them only a day or two before!

No. Mr. Henri hadn't seen the window-cleaner's name. But he thought it must be the same that his sister had. They could ask her.

"Well, we can go through all these, and see if any of them are *likely* to have taken the money," said Fatty. "But I think we can cross out the grocer's boy, for instance."

"Ah, no," said Mr. Henri. "He was in Hollies for quite a long time. It might well be he."

"Oh! Yes, you're right. We must go into every one of these names," said Fatty. "Well, I'll get the others to help. They'll have to do some real detective work, I can see!"

He drank his coffee and talked a little longer. Mr. Henri was now back on the couch, coughing rather a lot. "It is the excitement," said his sister. "He is really much better. Come and see him whenever you like, and ask him what you like. It is a puzzle he would like to solve!"

Fatty said good-bye and went. He was just walking home when he suddenly remembered that he had come on his bicycle. Where had he left it? Oh, yes, by Hollies. He went back to get it and wheeled it to the road.

A thought flashed into his head. The car had taken away the furniture last night! It must have stood just here, in the road outside Hollies' front gate. But now he was sure that it couldn't have been a car. It must have been a small van of some kind — perhaps a small removal van.

He looked down on the road. It was not a good road, and was muddy and soft just there. The marks of wheels were plainly to be seen.

"Ah!" said Fatty, pleased. "I'm a jolly bad detective lately! I nearly forgot to check up for wheel-marks! And here they are, under my nose."

The tyre-marks were big and wide — too wide for an ordinary car, Fatty decided. Much more like those of a small removal van. He got out his notebook and sketched the pattern left in the mud by the tyres. Then he measured them across and entered the figure down in his notebook. The tyre patterns were so plain that Fatty thought the tyres must be quite new. That might be a help.

Near by was a lamp-post, and a mark on it caught Fatty's eye. It was a straight brown mark, almost a cut in the white lamp-post. Fatty looked at it.

"That van might quite well have run too close to it," he thought. "Anyway, it's worth noting down. 'Van may be painted a chocolate-brown, and may have a scratch on

wing about two feet from ground.' Well, we're getting on
— I hope!"

He shut his book, put it into his pocket and rode off
with Buster in the front basket. He wanted to call a meeting
of the Five Find-Outers that afternoon. This *was* a mystery,
after all. And it needed getting down to, because there were
quite a lot of suspects.

"What a bit of luck that I went to look for Larry's
window-leather last night!" he said to himself, as he cycled
home. "If I hadn't gone and heard all that noise last
night and hadn't gone again to explore this morning, old
Goon would have had the field to himself. He wouldn't
have told us a thing. Now, as it happens, I know more than
he does!"

"Wuff," said Buster, agreeing thoroughly. "Wuff-wuff-
wuff!"

Fatty Tells Quite a Story

At three o'clock that afternoon Larry, Daisy, Pip and Bets
came along to Fatty's shed. He was already there, and on
the bench at one side were two or three sheets of neatly
written notes. Fatty was just reading them over.

"Come in!" he called, and the four trooped in. They
looked excited. Fatty had already telephoned to them to
say that there really *was* a mystery now, and they wanted
to know all about it.

"All sorts of rumours are flying round, Fatty," said
Larry. "Is it true that somebody took away all the furniture
in the middle of the night from Hollies Cottage — and the
old man was found lying on the floor because the thieves
even took his bed?"

Fatty laughed. "How do people get hold of these things?
83

It's true that the furniture went — but the old man slept peacefully all through the robbery, on his own bed. They didn't touch that. They did the job so quietly that he never heard a thing — snored all through it."

"How do you know that," said Pip, a little scornfully. "You weren't there!"

"Well, it so happens that I was," said Fatty, surprising the others very much. They stared at him.

"You were *there* — last night — when the furniture was all taken away?" said Larry at last. "Well, why didn't you stop them, then?"

"Because I had no idea what was being taken," said Fatty. "It was pitch dark, and they did the whole thing so quietly. But look — let me tell you everything in its right order — quite a lot has happened actually — and we've got to get right down to this, and really find out what's going on."

"Yes — but just let me interrupt for a minute," said Larry. "Did you find my window-leather? Mother was on and on about it this morning."

"No, I didn't," said Fatty. "I'm sorry about that, but honestly it wasn't anywhere to be found. All I hope is that Goon didn't find it."

"Well, he'd think it belonged to the woman who cleans out Hollies Cottage," said Daisy. "We'll just have to buy Mother another one, Larry."

"Blow!" said Larry. "That really was a silly idea of yours, Fatty — making me go and clean those windows."

"Yes, but remember that it was all because of that that we're in on this mystery," said Fatty. "It really began with seeing that old man crawling about jabbing at all his furniture — and then us going to collect your leather and hearing him yelling for the police."

"That's true," said Larry. "Well, all right, I'll say that a

84

very silly idea happened to turn out well — but that's as far as I'll go."

Fatty changed the subject. He picked up his notes. "Now, listen," he said. "I've written out a short summary of what's happened so far — just to get our minds clear, so to speak — and I'll read it. Then we'll discuss any clues, and all the suspects, and make plans. Ready?"

"Yes! This sounds good! said Pip, settling himself comfortably on a box.

"Well, get ready to use your brains," said Fatty. "Buster, sit still and listen, too. It disturbs me if you keep snuffling for mice in that corner. Sit, Buster."

Buster sat, his ears pricked as if he were quite ready to listen. Fatty went quickly through his notes.

"The mystery begins when Larry goes to Hollies to clean the windows. He saw the old man there, crawling about, poking at his furniture. We know now that he was looking to make sure that his savings were safely where he had hidden them — either the whole two hundred pounds in some particular chair or sofa, or divided up and put into different places: Possibly in some carefully prepared, hidden pocket under a chair or chairs."

"Oh, that reminds me!" said Daisy, suddenly. "Excuse me interrupting, Fatty, but our charwoman told me she knew the old man when he was younger — and he was an upholsterer, so he'd know very well how to make some kind of hidden pockets in furniture, wouldn't he?"

"What's an upholsterer?" asked Bets.

"Bets! You're a baby!" said Pip at once. "It's some one who makes chair covers and curtains, and stuffs couches and chairs and things — isn't it, Fatty?"

"Yes," said Fatty. "That's an interesting bit of information of yours, Daisy. Very interesting. The old man probably made himself quite a lot of hiding-places here and there in the upholstery of his chairs or sofas. I'll just add a note about it."

Daisy looked pleased. "It's a sort of clue, isn't it?" she said. "A very small one, I know."

"It all helps to fill in the mystery," said Fatty. "I always think of our mysteries as jigsaws. We've got a great many bits and pieces – but not until we fit them together properly do we see the whole picture. Now, then, I'll go on."

"We're listening," said Bets, happily.

"Well, we come next to when we all of us went with Larry to find the leather he had left behind," said Fatty. "And we heard the old man yelling for the police. He is certain that his money was in its usual place – or places – about midnight the night before, but in the morning it is gone. He doesn't discover that it's gone, however, until six people, at least, have been to Hollies Cottage for some reason or other."

"And all those six are Suspects, then, till we prove them otherwise," said Larry. "Good! Who are they, Fatty?"

"All in good time," said Fatty ."Don't keep interrupting. Buster, sit! There is NO mouse in that corner! "

Buster sat, looking as if he knew better than Fatty where mice were concerned. Fatty went on.

"We decided at this point that it was only a question of straightforward robbery, and that Goon would be able to deal with it," he said. "But last night I went to get Larry's leather, and as I told you, I arrived just about the time the car, or lorry, or van came to remove the furniture out of that front room."

"Extraordinary!" said Larry, unable to stop himself from interrupting.

Fatty went on to describe what he had heard. "Actually I *saw* nothing," he said. "And I didn't even know till this morning that the midnight visitors were taking away all the furniture. I didn't know that they might have a van or a lorry – I thought it was a car. I imagined they might be kidnapping the old man, but I both saw and heard him, fast asleep, on his bed in the back room."

"What did you *think* was happening?" asked Pip.

"I simply couldn't imagine!" said Fatty. "All I heard were a few thuds and bumps and pants and a whisper – and it was all over quite quickly, really. Well, I thought I'd better go back to Hollies early this morning, just to see if I could find out anything, and when I got there, I had quite a shock."

"Why?" asked Bets, hugging her knees. "This is awfully exciting, Fatty!"

"Well, I found Goon there, and the old fellow, of course, and Mr. Henri, that Frenchman you all thought was me in disguise. He's staying with his sister next door, as you know, and he heard the old man yelling for help again early this morning. So he went to see what the matter was and then called the police."

"Oh, so Goon was in on this pretty quickly!" said Larry, disappointed.

"Yes. But I wasn't much later in arriving," said Fatty. "And wasn't I amazed to find no furniture in that front room! Of course I knew at once what had happened, because I'd actually heard the men moving it last night – though I didn't tell Goon that, of course!"

"What happened next?" asked Bets.

"Nothing much. Goon went off, leaving Mr. Henri and me with the old man – and Mr. Henri's sister said she'd give him a room till one of his relations came along. So he's there now. I had a good look round Hollies, but couldn't see anything to help me. Then I went back to Mr. Henri, and got a proper list of the people he had seen going to the bungalow yesterday morning. They're the Suspects, of course."

"Let's have a good look," said Larry; but Fatty hadn't quite finished.

"I've only got one clue," he said, "but it *might* be an important one." He told then about the well-marked prints of the tyres in the mud outside Hollies, and showed them the pattern in his notebook.

"I *think* it must have been a small removal van," he said, "because the distance between the front and back wheels was rather more than there would be in even a big car. Oh! – and the car or van may be a chocolate-brown. There was a new brown mark on a near-by lamp-post, as if the van's wings had scraped it."

"Well, it seems as if we have got to tackle the Suspects," said Larry, "and look out for a chocolate-brown van which probably has new tyres of a certain pattern. We'd better all copy out that pattern, Fatty. It would be maddening to see a chocolate-brown removal van with new tyres – and not be able to check the pattern!"

"Yes. Well, will you make four tracings of the diagram in my notebook?" said Fatty. "I'll go on with the list of Suspects and we can discuss them. You can trace the markings while you're listening."

Fatty turned to his list of six Suspects. He read them out. "One – Lady with papers or magazines, dressed in red coat, and black hat with roses. Two – Window-Cleaner. Three – Grocer's boy, from Welburn the grocer's, red-haired, and was in the bungalow quite a time. Four – man with bag, came in car with number ERT 100. Five – well-dressed young man, who stayed for only a minute. And six – a young woman who stayed a long time."

"Quite a list," said Larry. "A window-cleaner, too! I wonder if he noticed how clean the windows were!"

"That's what *I* wondered," said Fatty, with a laugh. "I'm going to have a word with the old man about these Suspects; he may be able to give me a few more clues about them. Then we must tackle each one."

"I never much like that," said Bets. "I'm no good at it."

"Yes, you are," said Fatty. "Anyway, doesn't your mother have Welburn's for her grocer? You could hang about for the grocer's boy, and have a word with him when he brings your groceries. You and Pip could do that."

"Oh, yes!" said Bets, glad that Pip was to help her. "What about the lady with the magazines? Would she be the vicar's sister? It sounds rather as if it was somebody delivering the Parish magazine."

"Yes. I can easily find that out," said Fatty. "Mother knows her. I'll go and see if she was delivering at Hollies this morning. If so, she's not a Suspect, of course. But we can't afford to rule any one out till we've proved they're all right."

"And we can look out for car ERT 100," said Pip. "I wonder who the young man is – and that young woman who stayed such a long time."

"Probably the old man's granddaughter," said Fatty, shutting up his notebook. "She comes to clean for him. Pip, you and Bets get on with the grocer-boy Suspect. Larry, you finish these tracings, will you, and let us each have one. I'll go and find out a bit more about these six people if I can. Daisy, will you wander about with Buster, and see if you can spot that car – ERT 100, remember."

"Right!" said every one and got up. This was exciting. A mystery they could really work on! Now who, of all those six, was the thief?

Fatty gets Going

Fatty went straight off to Mr. Henri. His sister, Mrs. Harris, was quite pleased to see him. Fatty had excellent manners, and the Frenchwoman liked a boy who knew how to behave.

Soon he was sitting beside Mr. Henri's couch. "Well, have you come to ask me more questions?" said the man, in French. "We will speak in French, will we not? It is so much easier for me – and you, you talk French like a native! You are a most accomplished boy!"

Fatty coughed modestly, and restrained himself from agreeing whole-heartedly with Mr. Henri. "I just wanted to ask you a few things about our six Suspects," he began.

"Ha! Mr. Goon also asked me many questions," said Mr. Henri. "He is a stupid fellow; but he asks good questions. They are well-trained in this, your police."

"Oh," said Fatty, disappointed to hear that Goon had had the bright idea of questioning Mr. Henri too. "Blow Goon! Well, it can't be helped. Mr. Henri, who, of all these six people on our list, went into the bungalow – right inside, I mean?"

"All of them," said Mr. Henri. "The door could not have been locked. Every one turned the handle and walked in."

"What! The window-cleaner too?" said Fatty.

"Yes, he too," said Mr. Henri. "By the way, my sister says that he is the same one she has. He came to do her windows first, and then went to Hollies."

"Does she think he's honest?" asked Fatty.

"Perfectly," said Mr. Henri. "And a good cleaner. But you should see him and question him, Frederick."

"Oh, I will," said Fatty. "Decidedly. You told me too about the lady with the papers or magazines. I think she may have been the vicar's sister, delivering Parish magazines."

"So? I do not know what they are," said Mr. Henri. "But yes, the lady may have been of that type – she too went in, but she did not stay long."

"What about the well-dressed young man you said went in for a short time?" asked Fatty.

"Well, he came again, when you were there," said Mr. Henri. "You saw him – quite well-dressed. Did he not say who he was?"

"Gosh, that was the old man's great-nephew!" said Fatty. "He called him uncle, I remember. So he came during the morning, *too*, did he – before we got there – and afterwards as well. Very interesting! I'll find out where he lives and do a spot of interviewing."

"The young woman must have been the granddaughter who cleans and cooks for the old fellow," said Mr. Henri. "There was also the man who came in a car – that is all, is it not? Well, which do you suspect the most?"

"I don't know," said Fatty. "I really don't. The one I suspect *least* is the lady with magazines – but even so I'll have to check up. The worst of it is Goon has probably checked up too. That makes it more difficult for me. I mean – a policeman has the right to interview people. I haven't!"

Mrs. Harris came in. "You will stay to tea, won't you?" she said. "We are just going to have it."

Fatty shook his head most regretfully. "I'm awfully sorry. Nothing I'd like better. But I must go and do a spot of interviewing before Mr. Goon gets too far ahead of me."

He shook hands politely, thanked Mr. Henri, and let himself out. It was about a quarter to five. He was quite near the Vicarage. Should he chance his luck and go and see if the Vicar's sister was in?

Fatty decided that he would. So he cycled away quickly and was soon riding up the Vicarage drive. He saw somebody just by the house, kneeling on a mat, weeding. The Vicar's sister! What a bit of luck!

Fatty got off his bicycle and said good afternoon. The Vicar's sister looked up. She was a small, kindly faced woman, who knew Fatty's mother well.

"Ah, Frederick!" she said. "Do you want to see the Vicar?"

"Well, no, I really wanted to see *you*," said Fatty. "I won't keep you a minute. It's about that poor old man whose money has been stolen. I and my friends happened to be the first ones to help him when he discovered his loss. And . . ."

"Yes, I was *so* sorry to hear about that," said the Vicar's sister. "I had been to see him myself only that morning, left him the Parish magazine, you know – his granddaughter reads it to him – and he was sitting in his chair, quite happy, listening to the radio. It was going so loudly that I could hardly hear myself speak!"

"Did you see anything suspicious at all?" asked Fatty. "We couldn't see anything out of the way when we arrived there."

"No. Everything seemed just as usual," said the kindly-faced woman. "I just left the magazine, had a few friendly words and went. Such a pity to hide money in one's house – a real temptation to thieves."

"Yes," said Fatty. "Well, thanks very much. I didn't think you could help me really – but you never know."

"How did you know I called there yesterday?" asked the Vicar's sister, looking suddenly puzzled.

"Oh, I just heard that you did," said Fatty, turning his bicycle round. "Thank you very much. My kind regards to the Vicar and his wife!"

"*One* of the list of Suspects," said Fatty to himself as he rode away. "I felt sure that 'woman with magazines' sounded like the Vicar's sister. Anyway, it's quite, quite obvious she had nothing to do with the money. She didn't say if Goon had gone to see her – I suppose he hasn't, or she would have told me. Well, I should have thought he would have shot along to interview her, even though he knew she wasn't really a Suspect."

But Goon had not thought of the Vicar's sister. The description of the woman with the magazines had rung a different bell in Goon's mind. Aha! A red coat – and a black hat with roses! Didn't that sound like the woman who had sold him that ticket and read his hand? The woman who had actually seen that fat boy Frederick in his hand – and a Mystery also!

"There's more in this hand-reading business than anyone would guess," said Goon to himself. "Much more. I don't reckon that woman who read my hand has got anything to do with the theft of the money, but I'm pretty certain she's the woman with the papers who visited Hollies yesterday morning, so I'll go and interview her – and maybe she'll read my hand a bit more. Maybe she could tell me more about the Mystery she saw in my hand."

Poor Goon! He had no idea that his visitor, the woman in the red coat, who had sold him the Sale Ticket, had been Fatty in disguise! He cycled hopefully up to Fatty's house, and rang the bell. The woman had told him she was staying for three weeks with Fatty's mother, so she should still be there.

Fatty had just arrived back himself, and was washing his hands in the bathroom. He saw Goon cycling up the drive and was puzzled. *Now* what did Goon want? He dried his hands and slipped downstairs, going into the lounge, where his mother was sewing.

Jane came into the room almost at once. "Mr. Goon, the policeman, would like a word with you, Madam," she said.

Mrs. Trotteville frowned. She was not fond of Mr. Goon. "Show him in here," she said. "Don't go, Frederick. It may be something to do with you."

Mr. Goon came in, helmet in his hand. He was always on his best behaviour with Mrs. Trotteville. "Er – good evening, Madam," he said. "I wondered if I could have a word with the lady who is staying with you."

Mrs. Trotteville looked surprised. "There is no one staying with me at present," she said. "Why do you think there is?"

"But – but there must be!" said Mr. Goon, startled. "Why – this lady – she came to see me the other morning and sold me a ticket for a Sale of Work – five bob – er, five shillings I paid for it. She said she was a friend of yours and was staying with you for three weeks. I wanted to see her to ask a few questions. I have reason to believe that she was one of the people who went to Hollies – where the robbery was, you know – on the morning that the old man discovered that his money was gone."

Fatty turned round and poked the fire vigorously. How marvellous! How super! Goon really and truly thought that one of the Suspects was the woman in the red coat who had visited him and read his hand – Fatty himself in disguise!

"Really, Mr. Goon, I can't think why in the world this woman said she was staying with me," said Mrs. Trotteville, very much on her dignity. "I have never heard of her in my life!"

"But – but she sold me this ticket for five bob!" said poor Mr. Goon, in anguish. "Five bob! Is it a dud, then?" He pushed the ticket at Mrs. Trotteville.

"No. It is not a dud," she said. "I also have those tickets for sale."

"She read my hand too," wailed Goon. "And the things she said were true." He stopped suddenly. No, it wouldn't do to tell Mrs. Trotteville what the woman had said about a fat boy.

Fatty was having a violent coughing fit, his handkerchief to his face. His mother looked at him, annoyed. "Frederick, go and get a drink of water. Mr. Goon, I'm sorry not to be able to help you; but I do assure you that I have no friend who goes about reading people's hands. Some one has – er – deceived you. Still, you've got the ticket. You can always go to the Sale. There will be plenty of good things for you to buy."

Mr. Goon made a peculiar noise – half snort and half groan. He got up, said good evening, and stumbled to the door. That woman in the red coat! Who could she have been? Telling him fairy tales like that – making him stump up for a silly Sale of Work ticket! What a waste of money. All the same, she did warn him against that fat boy, and she did know that a Mystery was near. Strange. Most peculiar.

Fatty appeared in the hall. "Oh, are you going, Mr. Goon?" he said. "Do let me see you out. Very strange that that woman should have said she was staying here, isn't it? By the way, how are you getting on with this new Mystery? For Mystery it is! You no doubt have plenty of clues?"

Goon looked at him with a surly face. "Yes, I have," he said. "And one or two of them you won't like – Mister Clever! I told you you'd poke your nose into things once too often!"

"What exactly do you mean by that?" said Fatty.

"Wait and see," said Goon, rudely. Fatty opened the door and Goon marched out. Fatty called after him politely.

"Oh – er, Mr. Goon! Did that woman who read your hand warn you against a fat boy, by any chance? She did, did she? Well, take her advice. Beware of him!"

And Fatty gently shut the door on a most bewildered Mr. Goon. Now – HOW did Fatty know what that woman had read in his hand? Goon puzzled over that for a very long time indeed!

Mostly About Window-Cleaners

It was too late to do anything else that evening. Fatty decided that he would go and see the window-cleaner first thing the next morning, then he would go to Pip's at ten o'clock for the next meeting of the Five. By that time the others might have something to report, too.

"After the meeting I'll see if I can find that young man — the great-nephew," said Fatty. "And have a word with the granddaughter too. By then we might be able to see daylight a little. My word — fancy Goon going right off the track, and coming up here to trace a woman who doesn't exist — the woman who read his hand. Poor old Goon. He's got hold of a bit of jigsaw that doesn't fit!"

Fatty decided that he would dress up in old clothes the next day, find the window-cleaner, and pretend that he wanted some advice about going in for window-cleaning himself. He might get the man to talk more freely if he thought he was not being interviewed.

"I'd better go early, or he'll be off to work," thought Fatty, and arranged with Cook to have breakfast at an earlier hour than usual. He was up in good time and came down just as Jane brought a tray of breakfast for him into the dining-room. She looked in surprise at Fatty.

"My word! Are you going in for chimney-sweeping or something?" she said. "Where *did* you get those dirty old clothes? Don't you let your father see you!"

"I won't," said Fatty, and began on his breakfast. He propped his notebook in front of him as he ate, considering all the facts of the robbery and the removal of the furniture. Pity they couldn't find out where the furniture was — it would help matters a good deal!

96

He had the address of the window-cleaner. Mr. Henri's sister had given it to him. "Sixty-two, North Street, Peterswood. The other end of the town. Well, I'll be off."

Fatty didn't cycle. His bicycle was too expensive-looking to be owned by a young man who wanted a job at window-cleaning. He set off at a good pace, with Buster at his heels.

It took him about twenty minutes to get to the address. No. 62 was a smart little house, with a television aerial on the roof. Evidently window-cleaning was quite a well-paid occupation. Fatty walked round to the back door.

A man sat there, cleaning some boots. He looked up at Fatty and Fatty grinned.

"Hallo, mate! What do you want?" said the man, liking the look of this cheerful-faced fat boy.

"Just wanted to ask you if you could give me a few hints about your job," said Fatty. "I might like to take it up – if any one would teach me!"

He spoke in a rough kind of voice, so that the man would not suspect him to be any other than he seemed.

The window-cleaner looked him up and down.

"You seem a likely sort of lad," he said. "I might do with a mate meself. When are you free?"

"Oh, not for some time," said Fatty, hastily, marvelling at the ease with which one could get a job. He then began to ask the window-cleaner a few questions: how much did a ladder cost? Could one be bought second-hand? Were leathers expensive?

"Look here, if you want a job at window-cleaning, you come and be my mate," said the man, at last. "You and I would get on fine. Don't you worry about ladders and leathers – I'll supply those if you like to come in with me. You go home and think about it, and let me know."

"Right," said Fatty. "That's kind of you. I say, did you hear about that robbery at Hollies?"

"I should think I did!" said the man, taking up another

boot to clean. "Why, I was cleaning the windows that very morning! Funny thing was, though I hadn't cleaned them for a month they were as clean as could be! I told the old man that when I went in for my money. His granddaughter was there, ironing the curtains, and she seemed surprised to see me – said another window-cleaner had been along a day or two before, and hadn't asked for any money at all."

Fatty listened to this with great interest, hoping that Goon wouldn't get suspicious if he heard about the other window-cleaner!

"Have the police asked you if you saw anything when you cleaned the windows that morning – anything unusual, I mean?" asked Fatty.

"No. I haven't seen the police," said the man. "I've got nothing to fear. I've been a window-cleaner for years and every one knows me. Anyway, I couldn't have taken the money – the granddaughter was there all the time, ironing away!"

"Yes. That certainly rules you out," said Fatty, thinking that the window-cleaner was another Suspect to cross off. "Well, I must go. Thanks very much for your help. If I decide to be your mate I'll come right along and tell you."

The window-cleaner waved a shoe-brush at Fatty, and the boy went round to the front, untied Buster from the fence and walked back home. He was thinking hard.

Why hadn't Goon interviewed the window-cleaner? He had had time. Didn't he know who the man was? Well, he was one up on Goon over that. Another Suspect gone!

Fatty arrived at Pip's just after ten o'clock. The other four were sitting waiting for him in Pip's playroom. Fatty was surprised to see such long faces.

"What's up?" he said. "Bets, you look as if you're going to burst into tears!"

"Fatty, something awful's happened," said Daisy. "Simply AWFUL! Goon found that window-leather Larry used, and it had our name on it — Daykin! Mother always marks all her household cloths."

"Good gracious!" said Fatty. "If only I'd known that! I'd never have let that leather lie there so long."

"Well, we're in an awful fix now," said Larry, "and really I can't help saying again, Fatty, that it was a most idiotic idea of yours to tell me to go and clean windows. You see, Goon saw the name 'Daykin' on the leather, and he knows that my name is Larry Daykin, and he immediately leapt to the conclusion that one or other of us five had played the fool, and was the window-cleaner on the morning of the robbery!"

"Whew!" said Fatty, and sat down suddenly. "This is a blow!" He sat and stared at the serious faces of the others.

"Did he come up to your house with the leather?" asked Fatty.

"Of course he did," said Larry. "And what's more he took the leather away again, saying something about its being a 'piece of evidence' — whatever that may be. So Mother hasn't got it back yet!"

"And he had us in, Larry and me, and asked us outright if we had cleaned the windows of Hollies two mornings ago," said Daisy. "But fortunately we were able to say we hadn't, because, as you know, it was a day or two *before* that that Larry cleaned them — not the morning of the robbery. But we felt AWFUL! We *had* to say it was Mother's leather, of course, but we didn't dare to say that Larry had cleaned the windows with it two days before the robbery — we just kept on saying that we didn't clean the windows on the *robbery* morning."

"And *he* kept on saying 'Then how did this leather get into those bushes?'" said Larry. "He's most awfully suspicious about it. It's dreadful. I don't know what will happen when Dad comes home and hears about it. I bet he'll get out of Daisy or me that I was idiot enough to clean the windows two or three days before that robbery! He'll think I'm stark staring mad!"

"I'll go and see Goon," said Fatty, getting up. "I can put things right, I think."

"How?" asked Larry.

"Well, it so happens that I've been to see the actual window-cleaner who *did* clean the windows on the robbery morning," said Fatty. "Man called Glass – good name for a window-cleaner!"

Nobody could raise even a smile.

"Well, anyway, this fellow says he *did* clean the windows that morning, and when he'd finished he went into the bungalow, and the granddaughter was there – ironing curtains or something, he said – and she paid him his money."

"Oh, what a relief!" said Larry, looking more cheerful. "If Goon knows *that*, maybe he won't keep on trying to make me say I was there cleaning windows that morning too. Honestly, Fatty, I began to feel that he thought I'd stolen the money!"

"I'm sorry to hear about this, Larry," said Fatty. "I'll go and see Goon now."

He went off with Buster, leaving four slightly more cheerful children in Pip's playroom. Daisy got up.

"Come on, let's go out. I feel quite depressed. Let's have some ice-creams – always a good cure for things that make us feel miserable!"

Fatty went straight to Mr. Goon's. He saw the policeman's bicycle outside and was thankful. Mrs. Mickle answered the door.

"Mr. Goon in?" asked Fatty. She nodded and showed him into the office. The skinny little Bert stood slyly in the hall. Fatty gave him a look.

"Hallo, Skinny! BEWAAAAAAARE!"

The "beware" seemed to come from behind Bert, and reminded him of those awful voices he had heard a day or two ago. He looked behind him, gave a yelp and dis-appeared.

No one was in the office – but, draped over a chair-seat, was Larry's window-leather! Fatty's eyes gleamed. He spoke softly to Buster.

"Buster! Look – what's that? Fight it, then, fight it!"

And Buster leapt on the leather in delight, caught it in his teeth and dragged it round the room, shaking it and worrying it exactly as if it were a rat.

"Take it outside, Buster," said Fatty, and Buster obedi-ently ran into the front garden with it, growling most ferociously.

Mr. Goon walked into the room thirty seconds later, looking quite jubilant. Ha! He had got Larry and Daisy into a fine old fix. Larry was the window-cleaner, was he? Then he was one of the Suspects on the morning of the robbery. What would his father have to say to *that*?

But Fatty soon made him look a little less jubilant. "Oh, Mr. Goon," he began, "I thought it might interest you to know that I have this morning interviewed the window-cleaner who cleaned the windows of Hollies on the morning of the robbery – a man called Glass, living at 62, North Street, Peterswood."

"What?" said Goon, startled.

"He told me he cleaned the windows, then went into the bungalow for his money. The granddaughter of the old man was there, ironing, and she paid him. He couldn't have stolen anything under the very eyes of the young woman, so I should think we needn't consider the window-cleaner any further. What do you feel about it, Mr. Goon?"

Mr. Goon felt furious. He cast his eyes round for the window-leather – he would face Fatty with that and see what he would say! But where WAS the leather? He couldn't see it anywhere.

101

"Are you looking for something, Mr. Goon?" asked Fatty, politely.

"That leather," said Mr. Goon, beginning to be agitated. "Where's it gone?"

"Oh, dear, I do hope Buster hasn't got it," said Fatty. "He's out there growling like anything, Mr. Goon. Would you like to see what he's got?"

Mr. Goon looked out of the window. Buster had torn the leather to pieces! Nobody would ever have known that it had once been a most respectable window-leather.

"That dog!" said Mr. Goon, in a tone of such fury that even Fatty was surprised.

"I'll go and scold him," said Fatty, and went out. "By the way, you didn't thank me for coming to give you information about Mr. Glass the window-cleaner, Mr. Goon!"

Mr. Goon said the only thing he felt able to say — "Gah!"

A Talk in the Ice-Cream Shop

Fatty went straight back to Pip's house, but the others were not there. "I should *think* they've gone to have ice-creams," said Mrs. Hilton. "I believe I heard somebody mention the word!"

"Right. Thank you," said Fatty, wishing he had his bicycle. All this rushing about on foot would make him quite thin! "I'll go and find them, Mrs. Hilton."

He went off with Buster, who still proudly carried a small bit of the window-leather in his mouth. Fatty stopped at an ironmonger's in the main street, and bought a magnificent leather. It cost him sixteen shillings. He stuffed it into his pocket, and went on to the dairy.

The other four were there, eating ice-creams. They were

very pleased indeed to see Fatty's cheerful face.

"Is it all right?" asked Bets, eagerly, and Fatty nodded. He ordered a round of ice-creams for every one, and two for himself, as he was one behind the others.

"I went to see Goon," he said, "and I told him how I'd gone to see the real window-cleaner this morning. He was most annoyed."

"I bet he was!" said Larry. "He was just too pleased for anything to think he'd got *me* pinned down as one of the Suspects. But what about the leather? He's still got that. He'll come and flourish it at Daddy tonight, and make an awful scene."

"Buster, come here, sir," said Fatty, and Buster came. From his mouth hung the last bit of the window-leather. He wagged his tail.

"Well, well, well, if Buster hasn't taken it upon himself to remove that leather from Goon's office, fight it and chew it to bits!" said Fatty, solemnly. "Is that the very last bit, Buster?"

"Wuff," said Buster, and dropped it. Larry picked it up. "Yes," he said, "look! There's a bit of the name-marking on this corner — Dayk! Oh, Buster, you're the cleverest, cheekiest, best dog in all the world!"

"And he deserves a double ice-cream!" said Daisy, thankfully. "Oh, Fatty, I don't know *how* you do these things, but there's simply nobody like you for putting things right — going straight for them. . . ."

"Taking the bull by the horns, tackling the fury of the storm, putting the enemy to flight, and all the rest of it," said Fatty, grinning. "No, but honestly, I was really upset. Goon had something on us there; and you and Daisy could have got into a fearful row, Larry, all through my fault."

"But now Mr. Goon can't do anything, can he?" said Bets, happily. "He knows who the real window-cleaner was — you've told him — and he hasn't got the leather any more."

"And Mother's the only one who has suffered," said Larry. "She's lost her window-leather for good now!"

"Oh, I forgot," said Fatty, and pulled the brand-new leather from his pocket. He tossed it across to Larry. "A present for your mother," he said.

"Oh, *thanks*," said Larry, delighted. "Mother will be so thrilled that she won't say another word about Mr. Goon's accusations."

"Tell her he made a mistake," said Fatty. "And a bad mistake it was for him!"

"Fatty! Pip and I saw the grocer's boy when he came with the groceries last night," said Bets, remembering.

"Good for you!" said Fatty. "What happened?"

"Well, Pip and I kept biking up and down the drive, waiting for him," said Bets, "and he came at last, on his bicycle. Pip had let down his tyre so that it was a bit flat and he yelled out to the boy to ask if he'd lend him his pump."

"Good idea," said Fatty. "So, of course, you just fell into conversation. What did the boy say?"

"Not much," said Bets. "Your turn now, Pip, you tell."

"I asked him if he ever went to Hollies, where the robbery had been," said Pip, "and he was simply thrilled to tell us all he knew. But it wasn't much."

"Tell me," said Fatty. "Just in *case* there's something."

"Well, he went to the front door as usual," said Pip. "He knocked, and shouted 'Grocer.' Some one called 'Bring the things in,' and in he went."

"Who was there?" asked Fatty.

"The old man was there, with the radio on full strength," said Pip, "and a young woman, the old man's granddaughter. He said she called the old fellow 'Grandad.' She was very busy sewing something green. She told him to take all the things out of the basket and out them in the little larder. So he did."

"And that was all," said Bets. "He just stayed and listened to the wireless for a bit and then went."

"Yes. Mr. Henri said the boy was in the bungalow for quite a time," said Fatty. "That explains it. Well, *he* couldn't have taken the money either. The granddaughter was there all the time."

"Perhaps *she* took it," said Larry. "She had plenty of chance!"

"Yes. But why take it that morning when so many people seemed to be in and out?" said Fatty. "Anyway, we'll know better when we see her. She *sounds* a good sort, I must say, going up and looking after old Grandad like that. Still, you never know!"

Fatty took out his notebook, and opened it at his page of Suspects. "We can cross quite a few off," he said. He drew his pencil through "Grocer Boy." Then he crossed out "Window-Cleaner." He also crossed out "Lady with magazines."

"Oh, have you found out about her too?" asked Pip, interested.

"Yes," said Fatty, and told them. He also related how Goon had gone wrong, and had imagined that the lady with the papers, "in red coat, black hat with roses" must have been the funny old thing who had sold him Daisy's ticket for the Sale, and had read his hand – and how Goon had gone to Fatty's house to ask his mother if he might interview her!

Every one roared. "Oh! You had told him that you were staying with Mrs. Trotteville for three weeks, so he thought the woman must still be there!" giggled Bets. "Whatever did your mother say?"

"Oh, she soon put Goon in his place," said Fatty. "Poor old Goon – he's getting a bit muddled over all this! No, Buster, you can NOT have another ice-cream. That was a double one, in case you didn't notice!"

"Good old Buster — eating up that leather!" said Larry, patting him. "I must say it was a very fine way of getting rid of — of — *what* is it I want to say, Fatty?"

"A fine way of getting rid of incriminating evidence," said Fatty, promptly. "No, I'm not going to explain that, Bets. Use your brains."

"Who have we got left on the list of Suspects now?" asked Daisy, craning over Fatty's arm to see. "Oh, man in car, with bag — ERT 100. Fatty, I looked all over the place but I couldn't see any ERTs and I didn't see 100 either. Shall we stroll round again and look? I feel it must be a local person."

"Right. And then I think I'll go and interview the smartly dressed great-nephew, and find out what he wanted Great-Uncle for that morning," said Fatty. "He apparently went in for a very short while, and then came out, and, if you remember, he turned up again when we were there listening to Grandpa's laments about his money having been stolen."

"Yes. The granddaughter had left by that time," said Pip. "Where does this fellow live?"

"Mr. Henri told me," said Fatty, turning over the pages of his notebook. "Here we are — the old man told him the address, because Mr. Henri wanted to get in touch with his relatives — No. 82, Spike Street, Marlow. Apparently both he and the granddaughter live at Marlow — though at different addresses."

"When will you go and see them? Today?" asked Daisy. "Shall we come too?"

Fatty considered this. "Yes. On the whole I think it would be a good idea," he said. "Goon has probably interviewed them both by this time, and if they see me coming along full of questions, too, they may resent it. But if we all blow along, full of innocent curiosity, so to speak, we might do better."

"I can't go before lunch," said Daisy. "Nor can Larry.

We've got an aunt coming. We could meet you about three though, outside your house, on bicycles. We'll have tea at that nice little café in Marlow High Street."

"Yes. That's settled then," said Fatty, putting his notebook away. "Come on out, and we'll look for ERT 100."

They paid the bill and went out, Buster still with his tiny bit of leather. He growled at every dog he met.

"Don't be an idiot, Buster," said Fatty. "You don't really suppose any other dog wants your smelly bit of leather, do you?"

They looked at every single car they met, or that passed them. Not an ERT anywhere! They went to the car-park and examined every car there, which made the attendant extremely suspicious of them.

"What are you looking for?" he called.

"An ERT," said Fatty.

"What's that?" asked the attendant. "Never heard of it. There aren't no erts here, so you can go away."

"You're right," said Fatty, sadly. "There isn't a single ERT to be seen."

"There's Mr. Goon," said Bets, suddenly, as they walked out of the car-park. "Perhaps he's looking for ERTs too."

"No. He has other ways of finding out who owns any car," said Fatty. "The police can always trace any car by its number – and Mr. Henri is sure to have given Goon the number. Old Goon will be one up on us over the man with the bag and car ERT 100."

Buster ran out into the road, barking, when he saw Mr. Goon riding by. Goon kicked out at him, and nearly fell off. "That pesky dog!" he shouted, and rode on at full speed.

"Buster! You've dropped your bit of incriminating evidence," said Fatty, disapprovingly, pointing to the rag of leather that had fallen from Buster's mouth when he barked at Goon. Buster picked it up meekly.

They all went to Larry's house first. In the drive stood a car. "Hallo! — who's this?" said Larry. "Not our Aunt Elsie already, surely? No, it isn't her car."

A man came down the front steps of the house carrying a neat brown case. "It's the doctor!" said Daisy. "Hallo, Doctor Holroyd! How's Cook?"

"Much better," said the doctor, smiling round at the five children. "Well, there doesn't look to be anything wrong with *you*!" He got into his car, started the engine, and put in the gear-lever. He went off down the drive.

Bets gave a loud yell, and pointed. "ERT! ERT 100! Look, do look! ERT 100!"

So it was. "Gosh, to think we all stood here with it staring us in the face," said Fatty, "after hunting for it all the morning! Man with a bag too — why EVER didn't any of us think of a doctor?"

"We're not nearly as bright as we imagine," said Daisy. "Good old Bets! She spotted it."

"Shall you go and interview him?" asked Pip.

"No. I'm sure he couldn't help us at all," said Fatty. "He couldn't *possibly* have stolen the money — every one knows Doctor Holroyd! I expect he just went to have a look at the old man, and then shot away again in his car. All the same, we ought to feel jolly ashamed of ourselves not to have spotted the number, when it was right in front of our noses!"

"There's Aunt Elsie! Quick, Larry, come and wash!" said Daisy, suddenly, as a small car crept in at one of the gates. "Good-bye, you others!"

They fled, and the other four walked sedately down the drive. "See you at three outside your house!" called Bets. "Good-bye, Fatty. Good-bye, Buster! Hang on to your bit of — of — incriminating evidence!"

A Chat with Wilfred—and a Surprise

Every one was outside Fatty's gate at three o'clock, Buster included. "I'll have to put him into my bicycle basket," said Fatty. "Marlow's too far for him to go on his four short legs. Up with you, Buster!"

Buster liked the bicycle basket. He sat there happily, bumping up and down when Fatty went over ruts. He looked down on other dogs with scorn as he passed them.

It was about three miles to Marlow, and a very pleasant ride on that fine April day. They asked for Spike Street when they got there. It was a pretty street leading down to the river. No. 82 was the last house, and its lawn sloped down to the water.

The five got off their bicycles. "Put them by this wall," said Fatty. "Then we'll snoop round a bit to see if we can find the great-nephew – Wilfrid King is his name. We've all seen him, so we know what he is like."

They sauntered alongside the wall that ran round the little front garden of No. 82. They came to a path that led to the river. They went down it, looking across to the lawn that led down to the water.

They could see no one. They came to the water's edge and stood there. Then Fatty gave Daisy a nudge. A boat lay bobbing not far off, and in it a young man lay reading, a rather surly-looking fellow, in smartly creased grey-flannel trousers and a yellow jersey.

"There's Wilfrid," said Fatty, in a low voice. "Let's call out to him and pretend to be very surprised to see him. Then we'll fall into conversation. Remember we've just ridden over here to see the river – it's such a lovely day!"

Wilfrid, however, saw them before they could hail him.

He sat up and stared. "Aren't you the kids who heard my great-uncle shouting for help the other morning?" he said.

"Oh, yes! Why, you're Wilfrid, aren't you?" shouted back Fatty, appearing to be most surprised. "Fancy seeing you here! We've just ridden over, it's such a heavenly day."

"Did you meet that fat-headed policeman?" asked Wilfrid. "He's been over here today asking umpteen questions. Any one would think I'd robbed the poor old fellow myself!"

"Oh, has Mr. Goon been over?" said Fatty. "Do come and tell us. We think he's a bit of a fat-head too. But, really, fancy thinking *you* would rob your great-uncle. Poor old man! – I wonder who did."

"Ah!" said Wilfrid, and looked knowing.

"What do you mean – AH!" said Larry.

"Oh, nothing. That policeman wouldn't see a thing even if it was right under his nose," said Wilfrid. "I told him that it was I who kept on and on at my uncle, begging him to put the money into a bank. It's most dangerous to keep it in the house. Anyway, it appears that a lot of people visited Hollies that morning – there are quite a few persons who *might* have stolen the money!"

"Yes, that's true," said Fatty. "It's funny how many people went in and out all the time. Still, the old man's granddaughter was there most of the time, cleaning or something. She can probably clear most of the ones who came."

"Yes. She can clear me, for instance," said Wilfrid. "She was there when I went in. Marian's my cousin, and she and I don't get on, so I didn't stay long. She actually wanted me to help her with the work! Me! She said if I was going to stay long, I could jolly well put up the curtains for her, so I just walked out."

"Well, anyway, she can clear you, as you say," said Fatty. "It's a funny thing – she can clear most of the people

110

who went in and out, except perhaps the doctor and he doesn't really need to be cleared."

"Oh, is that so?" said Wilfred. "Have you got a list of the suspected persons? I'm there, too, I suppose."

"You can be crossed off if Marian, the granddaughter, can clear you," said Fatty, handing him the list.

"My word!" said Wilfrid, looking at it. "Six of us, and all crossed off except for Marian and myself."

"Yes. And you say that Marian can clear you, so you'll be crossed off too, soon," said Fatty. "Perhaps Marian has already seen Mr. Goon, and he's crossed you off."

"She's out for the day," said Wilfrid. "I told him that, so I don't expect he's seen her yet. I say, all of us will be crossed off – except one."

"Except one," said Fatty, watching Wilfrid as he bent his head thoughtfully over the list. "Did you know where the old man hid his money, by any chance?"

An angry look came over Wilfrid's face. "No, I didn't. He would never tell me. I thought that if only he would, I would take it and put it into the bank, but now it's too late. Somebody else has got it."

"And you think you know who?" said Fatty quietly.

Wilfrid hesitated. "Not for certain. I'd better not say any more. You're only kids, but you might go and say something silly."

"Yes. We might," said Pip, who had begun to dislike Wilfrid. It was quite apparent to them all that Wilfrid thought his cousin Marian had taken the money – but they couldn't help thinking that *he* would have had it, too, if he could!

"We must go," said Fatty, looking at his watch. "Well, I hope that Marian clears you, Wilfrid – it's rather important that she should!"

They went back to their bicycles and rode off to the little café they liked. Not a word was said till they got there.

111

They were early, so there was no one else in the room. They began to talk in low voices.

"It can't have been Wilfrid who took the money. If he and his cousin dislike each other, she certainly wouldn't have sheltered him if he *had* taken the money right in front of her eyes."

"So he can't be the thief," said Pip. "Well, then, who is?"

"It looks like Marian," said Fatty. "We'll go and see her after tea. What beats me is why somebody took all that *furniture* away the next night. I keep going round and round that, but I just can't see where that bit of the jigsaw fits into the picture."

"I can't either," said Daisy. "The furniture was cheap stuff – worth very little. *Could* the thief have imagined that the money was still there? No, I give up. It's a puzzle!"

They had a good tea and then went to call at Marian's house, hoping that she would be in.

"Here we are," said Fatty. "No. 5, Marlins Grove. Why, it's a little hotel!"

So it was – a small boarding-house, beautifully kept. The children rang the bell, and a neat, middle-aged woman came to the door.

"Is Miss Marian King in?" asked Fatty. "If so, may we see her?"

"I don't think she's in yet," said the woman. "I'll go and find out. Come into the drawing-room, will you?"

They all trooped in. An old lady was there, reading. She smiled at the children and nodded.

"Do you want to see some one?" she asked.

"Yes," said Fatty. "We'd like to see Marian King, if she's in."

"Ah, Marian!" said the old lady. "She's a sweet girl! Good to her mother, good to her old grandad – and good to tiresome old ladies like me. She's a dear."

"We know she used to go and do all kinds of things for

her grandfather," said Fatty, glad to have some information about Marian.

"Oh, yes! That girl was always thinking of him!" said the old lady. "Taking him up titbits she had cooked. Doing his washing and ironing. As particular as could be, she was. She told me she was going to take down, wash and iron his curtains last time she went – quite a job – and kind of her too, because the old man wouldn't be able to see them!"

"Yes, she did do the curtains," said Daisy, remembering what had been seen by the grocer's boy. "She must have been very fond of her grandfather."

"Oh, she was!" said the old lady. "She thought the world of him and couldn't bear him to live alone. And now I hear that the poor old man has been robbed of his money – dear, dear, Marian will be so upset!"

Fatty wondered why the woman who had opened the door had not come back. Had she forgotten they were waiting? He decided to go and find out. He slipped out of the room and into the passage. He heard voices at the end and walked down the carpeted hall-way.

Some one was crying. "I don't know *what* to say about Marian. First, that policeman comes to see her and I say she's out – now these children. Where *is* she? She's been gone for two days now! People will say she took the money! It isn't like Marian to do this. Oh, dear, oh, dear, I do so hope she's not come to any harm!"

Another voice comforted her. "Well, you do as you think best. Marian's a good girl, that I will say, and as for stealing money from her old Grandad – and she's so fond of him, too – why, that's nonsense. I do think you should let the police know tomorrow that she's missing. I do indeed."

"But they'll think she's run off with the money; it'll be in all the papers," said the first voice, sobbing. "My girl Marian, my only daughter, as good as gold!"

Fatty went back quietly to the drawing-room. He was

worried – and very puzzled. This was something he hadn't expected. Where had Marian gone? *Could* she have taken the money? Every one seemed to speak well of her – and yet – and yet – why had she gone away?

Fatty entered the drawing-room and spoke quietly to the others. "I don't think we'll wait." He turned to the old lady and spoke politely.

"If the maid comes back, will you please say we're sorry we couldn't wait? Thank you!"

The old lady nodded, thinking what well-behaved children these were. The five went out, and collected Buster from the post to which he had been tied. He was delighted to see them.

"Don't say anything now," said Fatty, in a low voice. "I've got some news."

They mounted their bicycles, and waited until they were beyond Marlow in a deserted country road. Fatty jumped off his bicycle. The others did the same. They went to a gate, leaned their bicycles there and gathered round Fatty, puzzled at his serious face.

"Marian has disappeared," he said. "I overheard her mother say so. They're terribly upset – half afraid she's gone off with the money, and worried about what the papers will say if they get to hear of her disappearance! What do you think of that!"

"Gosh!" said Larry. "It really does look as if she's the thief. After all, she's the one most likely to have wormed herself into the old man's confidence and got his secrets out of him – where the money was kept, for instance."

"Yes. There doesn't seem any other reason why she's gone," said Fatty. "Well, until she comes back, we can't get much further in this mystery. We don't know two important things – where or why Marian has gone, and where or why the furniture has gone. This is one of the most puzzling mysteries we've tackled."

"Yes. And I'm sure that NOBODY could solve it, even if they knew all we know," said Pip. "Well, let's get back. There's not much more we can do now."

So they rode back to Peterswood, disappointed and puzzled. Well, perhaps the simplest explanation was the right one: Marian had taken the money and gone off with it!

And yet – what about that stolen furniture! Could that have been Marian too? They gave it up!

"It's too mysterious a mystery!" said Bets. "Mr. Goon CERTAINLY won't solve it!"

An Extraordinary Find

Fatty was unusually quiet that evening. The five of them, with Buster, were down in Fatty's shed. Bets slipped her hand through his arm.

"What's the matter, Fatty? Are you worried?"

"I'm puzzled more than worried," said Fatty. "I really am. I CAN'T believe that the granddaughter Marian would rob an old man she had been looking after so lovingly. And yet I feel certain that Wilfrid hasn't got the money, and what's more doesn't know where it is."

"Then is there somebody else – a seventh person – that we don't know about?" asked Larry.

"I did wonder if there could be," said Fatty. "Some one who perhaps went round the *back* of the bungalow that morning of the robbery, and got in without being seen. Mr. Henri could see every one going in at the front, but not at the back."

"Yes. That's true," said Daisy. "Also, I suppose it *is* possible that he wasn't looking out of his window every minute of the time."

"That's so," said Fatty. "But I think the old man would have mentioned any one else. Mr. Henri had a good talk with him, and is pretty certain there was no one else."

"Let's have a game," said Pip, who was getting just a bit tired of all this talky-talk.

"No. You have one, and let me think," said Fatty. "I'm at my wit's end — and yet I feel as if there's some clue that would give me the key to the whole mystery!"

"Well, anyway, the money's gone," said Pip. "So has Marian. It's a bit fishy."

"Perhaps it's still at Hollies," suggested Bets. "In a place where nobody has looked."

"I hunted everywhere," said Fatty. "It's such a *small* place — there really is nowhere to hide anything, once you rule out the chimney and the floor-boards. There's no furniture now to speak of — just the old man's bed, a chair, and a little table in that back room. And a lamp, a stove . . ."

"That old fender," put in Daisy.

"And the curtains," said Bets. "They had to leave those, I suppose, in case old Goon came by at night and shone his torch in at the window. He'd have discovered the bare room then, of course."

"Oh, come on, do let's have a game," said Pip. "I know when I'm beaten. There's something peculiar about all this, something we don't know about."

Fatty grinned suddenly. "All right!" he said. "I'm inclined to think you're right. There are some bits of this jigsaw that we haven't got — it isn't that we can't fit them into the picture. We just haven't got them. Hand over the cards, Pip. You never shuffle properly."

When the others went, Fatty walked part of the way with them, Buster at his heels. It was a lovely evening, and looked like being a glorious day tomorrow.

They went round a corner in a bunch, and bumped into

a burly form. "Hey!" said a familiar voice. "Can't you look where you're going?"

"Oh, good evening, Mr. Goon," said Fatty. "Out for a little stroll? Solved the mystery yet?"

"Oh, yes!" said Goon. "No mystery in it at all – if you're talking about the Hollies affair, that is. Plain as the nose on your face. It's that girl Marian."

Fatty was thunderstruck. "What do you mean? Surely she didn't take the money?"

"You wait and see the papers tomorrow morning," said Mr. Goon, enjoying himself. "Thought yourself so clever, didn't you? Well, you're not."

"Has the money been found?" asked Fatty.

"You wait and see," said Mr. Goon again. "And look here – I bin thinking – do you know anything about that lady that read my hand?"

Mr. Goon looked extremely threatening and Bets promptly went behind Larry.

"Let me see now, which lady do you mean?" asked Fatty, as if plenty of people read Goon's hand.

Goon gave one of his snorts. "You're a pest!" he said. "But this time I'm on top, see? You watch the papers tomorrow morning!"

He went on down the road, looking very pleased with himself. Fatty gave a hollow groan.

"I do believe that fat policeman knows something we don't. Blow him! I'll never forgive myself if we let him get the better of us. It rather looks as if Marian is the black sheep."

"I thought she was," said Pip. "Going off like that. Perhaps they've found her, money and all."

"We'll have to wait for the morning papers," said Fatty. "Well, good-bye. It's sad to think this mystery is coming to an end while we're still in the middle of it, so to speak."

Bets squeezed Fatty's arm. "Perhaps something else will happen," she comforted him. "You never know!"

"It's not very likely," said Fatty, and gave her a hug. "Good-bye – see you tomorrow, all of you."

Fatty was down early the next morning to see the papers. There was nothing on the front page, but inside was a whole column. It was headed:

MISSING GIRL

AND

MISSING MONEY

It then went on to describe Hollies, the old man, the missing money, the sudden disappearance of the furniture, and now the disappearance of Marian! It didn't say that Marian had taken the money – but any one reading the news about the Hollies affair would immediately gather that Marian had taken both money and furniture!

"Now I suppose the hunt is on," Fatty thought. "Every one will be looking out for Marian. I suppose her mother told the police the girl was missing – or more probably Goon wormed it out of her and reported it. Gosh, I wish I could have been a bit cleverer over this mystery! I do feel that I've missed something, some clue, that might have been the key to the whole affair."

Fatty put down the paper and thought. "I'll go round to Hollies once more," he decided. "For the last time. Just to see if any bright idea comes to me. I'll go by myself without any of the others. I'll just take Buster with me."

He fetched his bicycle and rode off. He soon came to Holly Lane and went into Green-Trees to get the key. Mr. Henri still had it.

"The old man has gone to Marlow," he said. "They came to fetch him last night."

"Oh, and so I suppose when he asked for Marian and was told she was missing he made a fuss!" said Fatty.

"I'll tell you something he told me," said Mr. Henri. "He said that Marian knew where his money was. He had actually told her, and made her promise she would never, never tell anyone."

Fatty groaned. "So it looks as if she was the only one who knew — and I must say things look bad for her now. Well, if she took it, she deserves what's coming to her! May I have the key, Mr. Henri? I know I'm beaten, but I just want to have a last look round."

Mr. Henri gave it to him, and Fatty went off next door. He let himself in. The curtains were drawn across the windows, and the room was dark. He switched on the light, but it was very dim. He drew the curtains away from the windows and the sun streamed in.

Fatty remembered how Marian had washed and ironed the curtains on the morning of the robbery. "Surely she wouldn't have done that if she had been going to steal the money and clear out!" thought Fatty. "It doesn't make sense. In fact, nothing makes sense!"

He stood there, looking at the fresh, green curtains. He had his hand on the side-hem that ran from the top of the window almost down to the floor. It felt stiff and he rubbed it between finger and thumb.

"Funny," said Fatty, and felt the hem a bit higher up. Then he felt it round the bottom of the curtains. He held it to his ear and rubbed and squeezed. A faint crackle came to him.

Fatty suddenly grew excited — tremendously excited. He was filled with sudden exultation.

"I've found the money! I believe I've FOUND THE MONEY! Gosh, what a bit of luck!"

He took out his pocket-knife and ripped up the bottom hem of the curtain, cutting the stitches. The hem was now

119

loose enough for him to insert finger and thumb.

He felt about, and came across something papery. He pulled it out gently and stared at it, whistling softly. It was a pound note, rather dirty – a pound note!

"So that's where she hid the money – to keep it from Wilfrid, who had begun to suspect that it was somewhere in the furniture! He must have come and threatened her that he would search for it after she had gone that morning! And so she ripped open the hems of the curtains she was ironing, and sewed the money into them. What an idea!"

The curtain hems were packed with the pound notes. Fatty could feel them all the way round. He debated what to do about it. Should he take the money out? No, he might get into trouble. It would be perfectly safe to leave it there – nobody had guessed so far, and not a soul was likely to guess now.

"Anyway, no one will come here," said Fatty. "And what's more, I'll make certain they don't!"

He went out of the bungalow and locked the door. He put the key into his pocket. "I shan't take it back to Hollies. I'll just tell Mr. Henri I'll keep it – and ask him to keep an eye on any one who comes up to the front door. Wilfrid's got a key, that's certain, but I don't think he'll come again – and Marian certainly won't."

Fatty was so excited that he found it difficult to keep his news to himself. Finding the money had suddenly shed light on all kinds of things.

Marian had taken it. She had hidden it in the curtains to make sure that Wilfrid didn't find it if he hunted for hiding-places in the furniture. She hadn't even told the old man where she had put it, in case Wilfrid wormed it out of him – and the old fellow, looking for it after Marian had gone that morning, had thought it was stolen.

Why had Marian disappeared? Not because she had

120

taken the money. She hadn't! Had Wilfrid anything to do with her disappearance? It was almost certainly Wilfrid who had come with some kind of van or lorry that night and removed all the furniture. Why? Probably because Marian vowed that she hadn't got it, but that it was still hidden at Hollies.

"The pieces are fitting again," said Fatty to himself jubilantly. "If only I could find Marian – or the furniture. Would the furniture still be in the van? It would obviously be dangerous for Wilfrid and his helper to unload it anywhere. His people would be very suspicious to see furniture suddenly appearing in the house or in the yard. He probably had to leave it in the van."

Another thought struck him. "Perhaps Wilfrid's family are in the House Removal business! Maybe they have big vans, and it might be in one of those. Gosh, I'll have to find out quickly!"

Fatty could hardly get home fast enough. Quick, quick! He might defeat Goon yet, and solve the whole thing before Marian was arrested!

Night Adventure

Fatty rushed to the telephone directories in the hall as soon as he got home. He wanted to look up King's of Marlow. Were they Furniture Removers? They must be! He was certain they would be. Quick – he must find King's in the directory.

There were a good many Kings – A. King, Alec King, Bertram King. Claude King, Mrs. D. King . . . all the way down the list of Kings went Fatty's eager finger. At last he came to the end of them.

He was bitterly disappointed. Not one of the Kings was

a Furniture Remover. There was a butcher and a baker; but the Kings apparently did not go in for House Removals. Fatty stared at the list in despair.

"I'll go down it again, very, very carefully," he thought. "Now, then — A. King, Alec King, Bertram King, Butcher, Claude King, Dentist, Mrs. D. King, Edward King, the King Stables, Henry King ... wait now — stables! STABLES! That's it! That's it! Stables mean horses — and horses mean horse-boxes — horse-boxes means vans capable of removing furniture! I've got it, I've got it!"

Fatty threw the directory on the floor and did a most complicated jig up and down the hall with Buster flying after him, barking. He knew that Fatty was excited, so he was excited too.

Mrs. Trotteville suddenly came out from the lounge into the hall. "Frederick! What on earth are you thinking of? I have a meeting in the lounge, and you choose just this minute to act like a Red Indian."

"Oh, Mother! I'm so sorry," said Fatty, and in his excitement and jubilance he went up and hugged her. "But I've just made a great discovery, and I was celebrating it. So sorry, Mother."

"Well, go and celebrate down in your shed," said his mother. "And, by the way, please don't forget that your grandfather will be here by the eleven o'clock train. I want you to meet him."

Fatty stared at his mother in the utmost dismay. "Gosh, I'd forgotten every word about it! Oh, Mother — I can't meet Grandad! I'm so sorry."

"But you must, Frederik," said his mother, shocked. "I have this Committee meeting — and besides, you always do meet your grandfather. He is only coming for the day and would think it very rude of you if you go off somewhere. You knew he was coming."

Fatty groaned. "Yes, but I tell you I forgot every word

about it. I promise you I did, Mother. It isn't that I don't *want* to meet him or be with him – I do; but it just happens that I've got something very, very important to do, and it can't wait."

"Well, either it must wait, or you must get Larry or Pip to do it for you," said Mrs. Trotteville, in an icy voice. She went back to her meeting and shut the door.

Fatty stared at Buster, who had put his tail down at Mrs. Trotteville's annoyed voice. "That's done it!" said Fatty. "JUST when I'm really on to something. Edward King, the King Stables, Marlow – another bit of the jigsaw that was missing, and now I can't fit it into the picture because Grandad's coming. Why, oh why, did he have to come to-day?"

Fatty was very fond of his grandfather, but it really was most unfortunate that he should have to meet him and entertain him on this day of all days.

"The old man's furniture will be in a horse-box," he told Buster. "It might be discovered at any moment – but *I* want to find it, Buster. What a shock for old Goon if I produce both the money *and* the furniture!"

He debated whether to telephone Larry or Pip and tell them his ideas. "No," he decided. "If I get them to go over to Marlow and snoop about for a horse-box with furniture inside, they may make some kind of silly move and spoil everything. I'll have to put it off till tonight."

So Fatty went to meet his grandfather, and entertained him well the whole day.

"Any more mysteries?" asked the twinkling-eyed old man. "In the middle of one, I suppose? Well, mind you don't let that fat policeman – what's his name? – Goop – Goon – get the better of you!"

"I won't," grinned Fatty. "I'll tell you all about it next time you come, Grandad."

He saw his grandfather off at six o'clock that evening,

and then dashed round to Pip's. Fortunately Larry and Daisy were there too. Bets was delighted to see Fatty.

"Oh, Fatty! You do look excited. Has anything happened?" she asked.

"Plenty," said Fatty and poured out everything — the finding of the notes in the hem of the curtains — his idea about Removal Vans which now might be Horse-Boxes, or so he hoped — and his determination to go to Marlow that night and hunt for a horse-box full of furniture!

"I'll come with you," said Larry at once.

"You and Pip can both come," said Fatty. "We'll go and see the film called *Ivanhoe* at the cinema first — and then, when it's quite dark, we'll go hunting for horse-boxes!"

"Can't Daisy and I come?" asked Bets.

"No. This isn't a job for girls," said Fatty. "Sorry, Bets, old thing. You can't come to the cinema with us, either, because *Ivanhoe* won't be over till late — and you two girls can't wait about afterwards for us. We may be ages."

"All right," said Bets. "Oh, my goodness! — isn't it exciting? Fatty, you really are very, very clever. Fancy thinking of the curtain hems!"

"I didn't really," said Fatty, honestly. "I just happened to be holding a hem, and it felt — well, rather stiff. But it does clear Marian, doesn't it? She didn't take the money — she merely hid it from Wilfrid! Jolly good show!"

"Why did she disappear then, I wonder?" said Daisy.

"I don't know. That's a bit of the jigsaw I just simply can't fit in anywhere," said Fatty. "Still, we're getting on!"

The three boys cycled off to Marlow, after an early supper. Buster unfortunately was not allowed to go with them, as cinemas do not welcome dogs. He howled dismally when Fatty left.

Ivanhoe was exciting and the three boys enjoyed it. Along with the excitement of the film was an added feeling of delicious suspense — the thought of the "snooping" they meant to do afterwards! They didn't even wait to see the short second film, but came out into the clear night at the end of *Ivanhoe*.

"I've found out where the stables are," said Fatty. "I rang up and inquired. King's thought I wanted to hire a horse – but I don't! The stables aren't by the river: they are away up on the hill."

They lighted their lamps and cycled quietly along a country road. Soon Fatty turned to the right, up a steep hill. "This is the way," he said. "Good – here comes the moon! We shan't be in the pitch-dark tonight."

They had to get off their cycles because the hill was so steep. A private road branched off to the left and the boys walked up it. They left their cycles in the shelter of a hedge.

Buildings loomed up near by. A horse coughed. "These must be the stables," said Fatty, in a low voice. "Keep quiet and walk in the shadows."

Nobody appeared to be about. The stable-doors were all shut. A horse stamped occasionally, and one whinnied a little.

"Where do they keep the horse-boxes?" whispered Fatty. "I can't see any here."

"Look – there's another path up there, quite a wide one," said Pip. "Perhaps they're along there."

They went up the broad path. The moon suddenly shone out brilliantly and lighted every rut in front of them. Fatty stopped suddenly.

"Look – see those tyre-marks? Aren't they the same pattern as the one in my notebook, the one you copied, Larry? You ought to know – you made four copies!"

"Yes, they *are* the same pattern," said Larry and got out his copy. He shone a torch on it, though the moonlight was almost brilliant enough for him to read by. "Yes, it's the same. Goody! We're on the right track. Wilfrid must have taken a horse-box to remove all the furniture, and brought it away up here."

The path went on for quite a way and at last came out into a field. No horses were there just then, but the boys could see half a dozen in a field a good way down.

"Look – horse-boxes, and lorries, and carts!" said Pip, pointing. Sure enough, neatly arranged in a big corner of the field was a fine collection of horse-boxes. The boys went over to them.

"Look inside each one," said Fatty. There were four, and none of them was locked. The boys shone their torches inside; but to their great disappointment each horse-box was empty, save for a few bits of straw. Fatty was puzzled.

"Let's look at the tyres," he said. "Find a horse-box with newish tyres, the pattern clearly marked."

But none of the horse-boxes had four new tyres, and the patterns on them were not a bit the same as the one Fatty had seen outside Hollies.

The boys looked at one another. "Now, what?" said Pip. "Dead end, again!"

"Better look round a bit," said Fatty. "It is possible that Wilfrid hid away the horse-box with the furniture."

So they hunted round. They walked across the big field – and at the other side was a copse. Fatty saw a bridle-path leading into the bushes. He followed it, and suddenly came to a muddy piece where, plainly to be seen, were tyre-marks, and each of the three saw at once that they were the ones they were seeking!

Out came Fatty's notebook. "Yes! These are the ones! Come on, we're on the trail now!"

They followed the bridle-path, and then, neatly pushed into a clearing, they saw a small horse-box!

"Brown!" said Fatty. "And look – here's a scratch on the back wing where it scraped that lamp-post. *Now* we're on the track!"

The boys tried the door. It was locked. "I thought it would be," said Fatty. "Here, give me a shove-up, and I'll look in at the window. Half a mo – I've dropped my torch!"

He picked it up and flashed it on. Then Pip and Larry hoisted him up to look into the window of the horse-box. He saw that it was badly broken. He flashed his torch inside.

"Yes, the furniture is here!" he called, softly. "All of it! Hallo – wait – what's this!"

Before he could say any more to the others, a loud scream came from inside the horse-box. It so startled Pip and Larry that they let go of Fatty. He fell to the ground with a bump.

The scream rang out again. Then came an anguished voice. "Help! Oh help! Help me!"

"Who is it?" whispered Pip, scared. "We've frightened somebody. Let's go."

"No," said Fatty. "I know who it is. It's Marian! Gosh, she has been locked up with the furniture!"

Marian

Fatty rapped on the locked door. "I say! Don't be scared. Can we help you?"

There was a silence, and then a trembling voice came from the horse-box. "Who are you?"

"Just three boys," said Fatty. "Are you Marian?"

"Yes. Oh, yes – but how do you know?" said the voice. "I've been locked up here for ages. Wilfrid locked me in – the beast!"

"Whew!" said Fatty. "How long have you been there?"

"It seems as if I've been here for days," said Marian. "I don't know. Can you let me out?"

"I think I can force the door," said Fatty. "What a pity the window's so tiny, Marian — you could have got out of it."

"I smashed it, hoping some one would hear the noise," said poor Marian. "And I yelled till I couldn't yell any more. That beast of a Wilfrid got a horse and dragged the box into some safe place, where nobody could hear me."

"I'll soon have you out," said Fatty, and took out a leather case of finely made tools, small but very strong. He chose one and began to work at the door with it.

Something snapped. Fatty tried the handle and the door opened! A white-faced girl stood there, smiling through her tears.

"Oh, thank you!" she said. "I've been so miserable. What made you come here tonight?"

"It's a long tale," said Fatty. "Would you like us to take you back to your mother? She's frantic about you. And what about food? I hope you've had something to eat and drink while you've been kept prisoner."

"Yes. Wilfrid put plenty of stuff in the box," said Marian. "Not that I could eat much. He's a beast."

"I agree," said Fatty. "I suppose he kept on worrying you to tell him where your grandfather kept his money?"

"How do you know about all this?" said the girl, in wonder. "Yes, Wilfrid got into debt, and he asked my Grandad — his great-uncle — to give him some money and Grandad wouldn't. Wilfrid was very angry. He knew Grandad kept his money hidden somewhere, and he asked me where it was."

"And did you know?" said Fatty.

"Yes, I did," said Marian. "Grandad told me a little while ago; but often enough I've seen the old man grope about under this chair and that, when he thought I wasn't there, to feel if his money was safe. But I never told a soul."

"You remember that morning you washed the curtains?"

said Fatty. "Did Wilfrid ask you again for the money then – to tell him where it was?"

"Yes, and I told him I knew, but that I wouldn't ever tell a mean thing like him!" said Marian. "He said he only wanted to borrow some and he'd put it back later; but I knew him better! He would never repay it!"

"Go on," said Fatty.

"Well, that morning he said, 'All right, Marian. When you've gone I shall come back and hunt everywhere – and I'll find it, you see if I don't!" And I was dreadfully afraid that he would."

"So you were very, very clever and sewed the pound notes into the hem of the curtains!" said Fatty.

Marian gave a little scream. "Oh! *How* do you know all this? Surely Wilfrid hasn't found them? Oh, I've worried and worried since I've been shut up here. I wanted to tell Grandpa not to be upset if he couldn't find his money – I'd got it safe for him – but I didn't have a chance."

"It's all right. The notes are still inside the hems," said Fatty. "It was a brilliant hiding-place. Tell me what made Wilfrid come and take away the furniture?"

"Well, that afternoon Wilfrid came to see me at my home," said Marian. "He said he'd been to Hollies and Grandad was moaning and crying because his money had gone – and Wilfrid accused me of taking it. He said he'd get the police if I didn't share it with him!"

"Well, well, what a pleasant person our Wilfrid is!" said Fatty.

"I swore I hadn't got the money. I said it was still at Hollies, in the living-room, in a place he'd never find," said Marian. "And I told him I'd get it myself the next day and take it to a bank, where Wilfrid couldn't possibly get his hands on it.'

"I see. So he took a horse-box in the middle of the night, and went and quietly collected every bit of furniture from the living-room," said Fatty. "He meant to go through every stick of it at his leisure and find that money before you took it to the bank."

"Yes, but he couldn't find it because it was in the curtains, and he didn't think of taking those down," said Marian. "And oh, dear, when he went through the furniture and ripped it to pieces, he still couldn't find the money, of course, so he got me up here by a trick, pushed me into the van and locked the door."

"But why?" said Fatty, puzzled.

"Oh, he was quite mad, quite beside himself," said Marian, trembling as she remembered. "He said I could either find the money myself in the furniture, or, if I was lying, I could tell him where I'd hidden the money in my own home! And here I've been ever since, shouting and yelling, but nobody heard me. And each day Wilfrid comes to ask me if I've got the money, or will tell him where it is. He's mad!"

"He must be," said Fatty. "Cheer up, Marian, everything's all right. We'll take you back home, and tomorrow we'll deal with dear Wilfrid. Will you come up to the Hollies at half-past ten? We'll be there, and you can take the money out of the curtains yourself."

"Oh, yes, I *must* do that," said Marian. "How do you know all these things? It's queer to find you three boys here, in the middle of the night, telling me all kinds of things!"

"You walk along with us to where we've left our bikes," said Fatty, taking Marian's arm. "I'll tell you how we know – as much as I can, anyhow. Larry, take the number of this horse-box, will you?"

The boys took Marian back to where they had left their bicycles, passing the quiet stables as they went. Fatty told Marian a good deal of his tale, and she listened in amazement.

130

"Poor Grandad!" she said. "He must have been so upset. Never mind, he'll be all right when he gets his precious money back. How marvellous you three boys are – finding out everything like that. You're better than the police!"

Fatty took Marian back to her own home. "It's not so late as you think," he told her. "It's not eleven o'clock yet. Look – there's still a light in that side-window. Shall I ring the bell for you?"

"No. I'll slip in at the side-door and surprise my mother," said Marian. She gave Fatty a sudden hug. "I think you're a marvel! I'll be up at Hollies at half-past ten tomorrow morning without fail, with some scissors to undo the hems!"

She disappeared. Fatty waited till he heard the side-door open and shut softly. Then he and the others went to get their bicycles from the front hedge.

"Good work, wasn't it?" he said, with much satisfaction.

"My word, yes!" said Larry. "Gosh, I was so scared when I heard Marian screaming in the van that I let go of you, Fatty; you came down an awful bump."

"That's all right," said Fatty, in great good humour. "My word, what an evening! Who would have thought that Wilfrid would shut Marian up like that! He must be in great need of money to do such a thing. I have an idea that that smartly dressed young man is going to get into considerable trouble."

"Serve him right," said Pip. "He deserves it. I think Marian is a jolly nice girl. I *thought* she couldn't have stolen that money!"

They were now cycling quickly home. Pip began to feel uncomfortable. "I say!" he said. "*I'm* going to get into trouble too – being out late like this."

"I would, as well, if my people didn't happen to be out," said Larry. "You're lucky, Fatty, your people never seem to mind."

131

"I'm older than you are," said Fatty, "and wiser! If you get into trouble tonight, Pip, just say that something unexpected happened that you can't tell about, but that everything will be explained tomorrow morning."

"Right," said Pip. "What are you going to do now, Fatty? I bet I know! You're going to ring up Superintendent Jenks!"

"Quite right. Go to the top of the class!" said Fatty. "Well, we part here. See you tomorrow morning, half-past ten, at Hollies. Bring the girls too."

Fatty put away his bicycle when he got home and let himself in at the side-door. His parents were playing bridge in the lounge. Good, he wouldn't disturb them. He would telephone Superintendent Jenks from his mother's bedroom – where there was an extension – not from the hall. He could say what he liked there.

He tiptoed to his mother's room and shut the door. He went to the telephone and gave Police Headquarters number. A voice answered almost immediately.

"Police station here."

"Is Superintendent Jenks in?" asked Fatty. "If not, I'll ring his private number. It's important."

"He's not here. I'll give you his private number," said the voice. "Banks, 00165."

"Thank you," said Fatty and rang off. He telephoned again and got the private number. He heard the Superintendent's voice almost at once.

"Yes. What is it?"

"Frederick Trotteville here," said Fatty. "First of all, my hearty congratulations, sir, on your promotion!"

"Thanks, Frederick," said the Superintendent, "but I don't imagine that you're ringing me up at almost midnight just to tell me that."

"No, sir," said Fatty. "The fact is, we've done a bit of work on that Hollies affair."

132

"Hollies affair? Oh, yes, the old man whose money was stolen, whose furniture disappeared, and then the grand-daughter vanished – am I right?" said the Super.

"Quite right, sir," said Fatty. "Er ..."

"Wait now," came the Super's voice, "let me hazard a guess, Frederick. You've found the money, you've located the furniture, and you've got the girl! Am I right?"

"Well, yes, sir," said Fatty, with a laugh. "How did you know?"

"Oh, I had a report in two days ago from Goon, in the course of which he complained that Master Frederick Trotteville was greatly hampering the course of justice," chuckled the Superintendent. "I imagined that meant you were getting on with the case a lot better than he was. Actually he said that it was pretty certain the girl had gone off with the money, and should be arrested as soon as found."

"Did he? Well, he's not quite right," said Fatty. "Would you care to come along to Hollies, the bungalow where all this happened, at half-past ten tomorrow morning, sir, and I'll have the whole affair neatly tied up for you."

"Right, I'll be there," said the Super. "I was coming over anyhow to see what was happening. I didn't like the dis-appearance of the girl – from all accounts she's a good girl. I hope you will produce her, Frederick."

"I hope to, sir," said Fatty, trying to sound modest. "And –er – will Mr. Goon be there?"

"Of course! I'll have a message sent to him," said the Super. "Well, well, I don't know why we don't leave all our local affairs to you, Frederick. How's little Bets? Is she in on this too?"

"Oh, yes. We all are," said Fatty. "Right, sir. We'll all be up at the Hollies at half-past ten. Good night!"

Fatty put down the telephone, and rubbed his hands glee-fully. Good, good, good! He was about to do a delighted jig round the room when he stopped. No – his mother's bedroom was just over the lounge – it would cause quite a lot of trouble for Fatty if some one came up to hunt for the elephant stamping round the room above!

"I'll go and find old Buster," he thought. "I can hear him scraping at my bedroom door now. I'm coming, Buster. Good news, old thing! Get ready to bark your head off, Buster. Hurrah!"

Quite a Pantomime

Quite a lot of people walked up Holly Lane the next morning. Fatty, Larry, Daisy, Pip and Bets went first, talking excitedly. Bets and Daisy had been tremendously thrilled the night before when Pip and Larry had crept in to tell them the news of the Marlow adventure.

Fatty went up the front path, took the key from his pocket and unlocked the door. Mr. Henri, at the window next door, saw them, and left his couch. In a minute or two he was walking up the path.

"Good morning!" he said. "You did not leave me the key. Frederick, and that young man – what is his name? – ah, yes, Wilfrid – he was annoyed to find I did not have it. He said he had forgotten his own key, and wished to enter Hollies to see that all was right."

"Oh, he did, did he?" said Fatty. "Thought he'd have one more hunt round, I suppose. Good thing he didn't."

"He is coming back again soon," said Mr. Henri.

"Good! Couldn't be better," said Fatty. "The more the merrier. Would you like to stay, Mr. Henri? There is going to be a bit of a do here soon – you might enjoy it. After all, you've been in this affair almost from the beginning."

"I stay with pleasure," said Mr. Henri, beaming, "Ah, who comes now?"

134

"It's Marian!" said Fatty. He darted to the door to meet her. She looked much better now. She smiled round at the others. Then she saw the empty room.

"Oh, how queer it looks without the furniture!" she said. Her eyes went to the curtains. She put out a hand and felt one of the hems. Fatty smiled at her.

"Jolly good hems, aren't they?" he said. "Marian, I wonder if you'd be sweet enough to go and sit in the back bedroom till we call you. I want to produce you as a sort of — well, sort of surprise."

"Yes. I'll go," said Marian. "But let me leave the door open. I want to hear everything."

"You're setting the scene as if a play was going to be acted!" said Bets, giggling.

"Well, a play *is* about to be acted," said Fatty. "Now, who's this?"

It was Mr. Goon. He looked a bit puzzled as he rode up to the gate. He got off his bicycle, wheeled it up to the front door and put it against the wall.

Fatty opened the door for him. "Welcome!" he said. Mr. Goon scowled.

"What are you doing here?" he said. "You'd better clear orf. The Superintendent's coming. He wants particularly to talk to me about this here case. I've got all my notes with me, so just you clear orf. And keep that dog away from my ankles, or I'll report him to the Super."

"Sit, Buster," said Fatty. "My word, Mr. Goon, what a sheaf of notes you've got! Wonderful work! Have you solved the mystery?"

"No mystery about it," said Goon, scornfully. "That girl went off with the money — *and* the furniture. I'll soon have my hands on her. I've had information where she is."

"Really?" said Fatty. "Anywhere in this district?"

Goon snorted. "No! Miles away! Anyway, I'm not saying any more. You're not going to pick my brains. Me and

135

the Superintendent are going to have a good talk, and you'd better clear out before he comes. Get along, now!'"

"Here he is," said Fatty, as a sleek, black police-car drew up at the gate, and the Superintendent got out with a plain-clothes man behind him. Bets tore out to meet him. He swung her up into the air.

"If it isn't young Bets! Well, well, how nice to see you again! Well, Daisy, how are you? Larry, Pip, Frederick, you all look very merry and bright."

"I told them you were coming, sir, but they wouldn't buzz off," said Goon, hoping that the Superintendent would take the hint and send the five away. But he didn't. He asked who Mr. Henri was, and Fatty explained.

Goon rustled his sheaf of notes and coughed. The Superintendent turned and looked at him sharply.

"Got something to say, Goon?" he inquired.

"Well, sir, yes, of course, sir," said Goon, looking hurt. "I supposed you wanted to see me about this Hollies case, sir. If you could just send these kids away . . ."

"Oh, no. They may have something to say that would help us, Goon," said his chief. "They may even know a few things that we don't know!'"

Goon looked most disbelieving. "There's really not much to this case, sir," he said. "Just a bad girl who robs her old grandfather of his money, gets away with his furniture, too, and does a disappearing act."

"But I thought she was a girl of very good character, Goon," said the Super. "Girls like that don't suddenly do wicked things. How do we know she stole the money, any-way?"

"She didn't," said Fatty, to Goon's surprise. "Nobody stole it."

"You're potty," said Goon, quite forgetting himself. "Where's this money then, if nobody stole it?"

"The girl hid it," said Fatty. "She was afraid her cousin
136

Wilfrid would get it if she didn't put it somewhere safe."

"Pah!" said Goon. "What a tale! I'll believe that if you show me where she hid the money!"

"Right," said Fatty, and stepped to the curtains. He put his finger and thumb into the hem whose stitches he had snipped the day before, and pulled out a pound note. He displayed it to Goon, Mr. Henri and Superintendent Jenks. They all stared in surprise, and Goon gaped, his mouth open in amazement.

· "See – a pound note!" said Fatty, and took another from the hem, rather as if he were doing a conjuring trick. "The hems of the curtains are full of these notes – a first-class hiding-place. You remember that Marian, the girl, was washing and ironing curtains, don't you, on the morning of the supposed robbery, Mr. Goon? Well, Wilfrid came and threatened to look for the money when she had gone, if she didn't give it to him then and there..."

"And she was scared he'd find it, so she took it from its hiding-place – wherever that was – and undid the curtain-hems to make a new hiding-place!" said the Superintendent. "Sewed them all up again too. A most ingenious girl, this Marian."

Mr. Goon swallowed two or three times. He could find nothing at all to say. Mr. Henri laughed in delight.

"Very neat," he said. "And now will you tell us where the lost furniture is, yes?"

"Pah!" said Goon, unable to stop himself.

"What did you say, Goon?" asked his chief. "Can *you* tell us where the furniture is?"

"No. And nobody can!" said Goon. "Nobody saw it go, nobody knows who took it, nobody knows where it is. I've had it searched for everywhere!"

"Frederick, can you throw any light on this subject?" asked the Superintendent.

"Yes," said Fatty. "Wilfrid and another man came at midnight and carried it out piece by piece."

"Gah!" said Goon. "Anybody would think you were there!"

"Well, as it happened, I was," said Fatty. "It was taken away in a horse-box — got the number, Larry? Yes, OKX 143 — and it is now in that same horse-box, rather the worse for wear, in a copse near the stables belonging to King's, in Marlow. I can take you there any time you like, Mr. Goon."

"You've got the money, you've got the furniture, but you haven't got the girl!" said Goon. "And I've had information where she is!"

"That's clever of you, Mr. Goon," said Fatty. "You tell me where *you* think she is — and I'll tell you where *I* think she is!"

"I have information here that she's gone across to Ireland," said Mr. Goon.

"And I have information that she's in the next room," said Fatty, with a grin. "Marian! Are you there?"

And to Mr. Goon's undying amazement Marian walked shyly into the room! Mr. Henri gave an exclamation. He had wondered who Marian was. The Superintendent glanced at his amazed plain-clothes officer and winked.

"Quite a pantomime!" he said, and the plain-clothes man grinned and nodded. He moved forward and asked Marian a few questions. Where had she been since she disappeared? Why had she gone away? He wrote down her answers rapidly, while Goon listened in the utmost astonishment.

"I understand, then, that these three boys found you locked up in the horse-box last night?" he said. "And that your cousin Wilfrid was responsible for detaining you there?"

"Here, wait a minute!" said Goon, unable to believe his ears. "You say these kids found her in that horse-box. How did *they* know about it? Why wasn't *I* told?"

"Frederick telephoned me last night," said his chief. "Quite rightly, too. It is possible that you might not have believed him, Goon."

Goon collapsed. His face went slowly purple and he turned and looked out of the window. That boy! That Toad of a boy!

"And now all we want to complete the merry little company is our friend Wilfrid," said the Superintendent. "I imagine that even *you* can't supply him, Frederick?"

Fatty was about to say sorrowfully that no, he was afraid he couldn't, when he heard the front-gate click. He looked out of the window and saw – Wilfrid!

Yes, Wilfrid had chosen that moment to come back and hunt round once again for the money. He saw that the door was now open and hurried to go inside. He stepped over the threshold – and stopped abruptly. The plain-clothes man moved casually beside him.

"Oh!" said Wilfrid, "What's all this? Something happened?" Then he saw his cousin, and went very white.

"Marian! What are you doing here?"

"You thought I was still in the horse-box, didn't you?" said Marian. "Well, I'm not. I'm here. I've come to get the money of Grandad's I hid away – see, in the hem of the curtains! You won't get it, Wilfrid! You won't have it to pay your bills!"

Wilfrid stared at the notes that Marian was pulling out of the curtain-hem. He ran his hand over his forehead. Then he made a sudden backward dart for the door.

But the plain-clothes man was there, and a hand with fingers of steel gripped Wilfrid's arm and held him fast.

"Don't go yet, Wilfrid," said the Superintendent. "There are quite a lot of questions we want to ask you."

His voice was suddenly different from the merry, kindly voice that the children were used to. Bets shivered a little. The Super was their friend, their very good friend, but to people like Wilfrid he was an implacable enemy, stern and unyielding. Wilfrid stood before him, as white as a sheet, trembling from head to foot.

"Johns – you and Goon stay here and let him tell you about the midnight move," said the Superintendent. "Where he parked the van and everything. Then take him along to the police station. I'll be there in an hour."

"Right, sir," said Johns, the plain-clothes man. Goon muttered something, but nobody could catch what he said. Still, as nobody listened, it didn't matter! Poor Goon, he looked very downcast as the five children and Marian went away with the Superintendent.

Mr. Henri went with them and said good-bye at the gate. "I have such a story to tell to my sistair," he said. "Please to come and see us soon! Au revoir!'"

"Where are we going?" asked Bets, hanging on to the burly Superintendent's arm.

"Well, isn't there some place here that sells ice-creams and macaroons?" said the big man. "I had an early breakfast – and I don't often see you. I'd like to stand you all a treat this morning – Marian too! She looks as if she wants feeding up a bit! Been starved in that horse-box, I expect, Marian!'"

"I couldn't eat very much," she said. "But I'm quite all right now, thank you. So is my mother. She was *so* thankful to see me. I'd still be a prisoner if it wasn't for these three boys!'"

"Ah, here is the place I mean," said the Superintendent, stopping outside the spotlessly clean dairy. "Yes. Best macaroons I ever had in my life came from here. In we go!'"

And in they went, Buster too, much to the surprise of the

little diary-woman, who didn't expect quite so many customers all at once — seven — and a dog who was as good as a customer any day, because he was just as fond of macaroons and ice-creams as the children were!

"Er — twenty-one macaroons, please. Oh, I beg your pardon, Buster — twenty-four, I mean," said the Superintendent. "And a first round of eight ice-creams — and orangeade for everyone but the dog."

"Yes, sir," said the dairy-woman, and hurried away. She brought the orangeade at once. "The other things are just coming," she said.

The Superintendent lifted his glass. "Let us drink to the day when Frederick Trotteville becomes my right-hand man!" he said. Fatty blushed with pride, and they all drank heartily.

Then Fatty lifted his glass. "To my future chief, Superintendent Jenks!" he said, and everyone again drank heartily. Now, only the Superintendent had any orangeade left.

"Ah, can't waste it!" he said. "To the Five Find-Outers — and Dog. Many Happy Mysteries!"

Yes, we all wish them that. Many more mysteries — and may each one be more mysterious than the last!

Outstanding fiction from the Granada Children's list.

INVISIBLE MAGIC   Elisabeth Beresford   60p ☐

What happens when a modern boy *half*-releases a centuries old spell.

DANGEROUS MAGIC   Elisabeth Beresford   60p ☐

Sammy and Eleanor pledge themselves to help the Unicorn get back to its own Place and Time. But where is that? And when?

THE BIG TEST   Roy Brown   50p ☐

A fast-moving adventure story set in the streets around London's Oval cricket ground on the last day of the Test.

A NAG CALLED WEDNESDAY   Roy Brown   50p ☐

When Liz and Larry 'find' a horse wandering the London streets, they think that keeping it will be easy. A funny and exciting chase story.

ROBIN HOOD   Antonia Fraser   40p ☐

The adventures of the fabulous hero in a stirring retelling.

NO PONIES FOR MISS POBJOY
       Ursula Moray Williams   50p ☐

The girls of Canterdown were mad on horses. Their new head-mistress cared only for cars — and for passing exams. A hilarious school story with a difference.

THE HOUSE IN CORNWALL   Noel Streatfield   35p ☐

A west country holiday with an unknown uncle could be fun. Or it could be dismal. Edward, Sorrell and Wish certainly were to find it surprising — and dangerous.

THE WINTER OF ENCHANTMENT
       Victoria Walker   20p ☐

A magic mirror transports Sebastian from his Victorian world of winter snow to the magic world of Melissa, Mantari and the wicked enchanter.

ENID BLYTON is Granada's bestselling children's author. Her books have sold millions of copies throughout the world and have delighted children of many nations. Here is a list of her books available from Granada Children's Books.

MYSTERY OF THE BANSHEE TOWERS	75p	☐
MYSTERY OF THE BURNT COTTAGE	75p	☐
MYSTERY OF THE DISAPPEARING CAT	75p	☐
MYSTERY OF THE HIDDEN HOUSE	75p	☐
MYSTERY OF HOLLY LANE	75p	☐
MYSTERY OF THE INVISIBLE THIEF	75p	☐
MYSTERY OF THE MISSING MAN	75p	☐
MYSTERY OF THE MISSING NECKLACE	75p	☐
MYSTERY OF THE PANTOMIME CAT	75p	☐
MYSTERY OF THE SECRET ROOM	75p	☐
MYSTERY OF THE SPITEFUL LETTERS	75p	☐
MYSTERY OF THE STRANGE BUNDLE	75p	☐
MYSTERY OF THE STRANGE MESSAGES	75p	☐
MYSTERY OF TALLY-HO COTTAGE	75p	☐
MYSTERY OF THE VANISHED PRINCE	75p	☐

All these books are available at your local bookshop or newsagent, or can be ordered direct from the publisher. Just tick the titles you want and fill in the form below.

Name ....

Address ....

....

Write to Granada Cash Sales, P.O. Box 11, Falmouth, Cornwall TRIO 9 EN. Please enclose remittance to the value of the cover price plus:
UK: 30p for the first book plus 15p for the second book plus 12p per copy for each additional book to a maximum charge of £1.29. BFPO and EIRE: 30p for the first book plus 12p per copy for the next 7 books, thereafter 6p per book.
OVERSEAS: 50p for the first book and 15p for each additional book.
Granada Publishing reserve the right to show new retail prices on covers, which may differ from those previously advertised in the text or elsewhere.